That's All.

For little Sophie.

Chapter One

July 14th 2014.

06.45pm

I wreaked of ignorance. We boarded the train and sat in the seats beside the only open window. I was wearing the most formal outfit I had worn all summer- a woollen, cropped, pink jumper and jeans. I had nicer clothes packed in my bag, but anything beyond jeans and a hoodie seemed very ambitious. Either way, the 5pm train from Heuston to Westport didn't feel like much of a special occasion.

Having never set foot out of the city of Dublin, apart from flying abroad, I was imagining drinking in sheep filled fields with Aran- clad locals.

The few native Irish people that still populated Dublin city are quite proud of the fact that in most people's minds, Ireland's chief exports are Irish people, potatoes, and playwrights - I wondered what the folks in Mayo would be like. Despite the fact that Ireland as an Island over the last 7,000 years has been invaded by the Celts, the Vikings, the Normans, the British, and Japanese tourists, and was adapting to new diverse cultures, I had an image in my head that Mayo was populated by 100% Irish people, and would drastically contrast to the modern "Dublin" which we were leaving.

Conversation was strained with Anna on the three-hour train journey, as she was still somewhat mourning a recent breakup and couldn't quite shake the image of her naked boyfriend's sweaty face kissing his "just a friend" work colleague, who we had just begun to grow close to this summer.
"Anna,"
She barely glanced up in response, bored of my company, and most likely tired of my futile attempts to break the silence.
 "Stop stalking his profile".
I snatched the phone from her grasp and was admittedly quite proud to discover she was in fact scrolling through my playlist in an effort to pass the time rather than listen to my pathetic attempts to distract her from her mood.
"How long has it been now?" I enquired, already

knowing the answer.

"Seven weeks"

"So what are you going to do about it?"

"Hold a funeral for my sex life."

As she retrieved her phone and put her earphones in, I decided this was the perfect time to return to my charade of pretending to be asleep and switch off conversation for the time being. I spent the rest of the journey thinking of better ways to cheer her up, and trying to expand my image of Westport beyond the stereotypical rural scene in my head.

July 14th 2014.

9pm

Jessica was waiting for us at the other end, and seemed overly excited to see us. Starved of company her own age, and driven mad by the silence of her country hometown, she launched straight into describing the weekend that lay ahead of us.

Jessica warned us to make sure to get an early night, as the prepping and pampering for the races the following

5

day apparently began before nine.

I couldn't help but picture the scenes of "The Races" and the attire that would go with it. I would inevitably have to wear a dress unsuited to the Irish weather, sip champagne and have meaningless conversation with well-to-do people who earned more money than they could count and were left with no other way left of spending it other than betting on innocent oblivious animals. Despite the hints of cruelty and privilege – I was grateful for Jessica's generosity and was ashamed to admit I was rather excited deep down.

July 14th 2014.

11pm

I had become far worse at socialising than I realised. That night, I found myself wearing the same clothes I had travelled in earlier that day, sitting in a pub with generic live Irish music and warm beer, surrounded by two of my best friends, yet alone, as they were being entertained by different boys. I zoned out and listened to the live music and made the decision to switch my pint for something stronger.

"Can I buy you a drink?"

His words were slurred and the smell of stale alcohol was just about bearable.

"I'm sure you can, but I'm enjoying this one, thanks"

"Alright, would ye get up and sing for us?" he teased.

My inner south side soul held back at the blatant opportunity to mock such a cringe-worthy Irish invitation.

He was handsome, and I wasn't sure what he was playing at, or if he was serious, but his intentions seemed innocent enough.

"I'll definitely need more than alcohol to make me do something like that"

"Which brings me back to my first question"

I knew what his intentions were, and I took the opportunity to take advantage of them. I accepted his offer of a vodka and coke. I shouldn't have been surprised when both types of coke were provided.

The evening ended with my decline of an invitation back to this married lawyer's apartment, and a disappointed Jessica with our hasty 3am departure.

July 15th, 2014
08.30am

A thick pounding under my skull and a sharp pressing on
my bladder forced my early morning trip to the
bathroom.

Hungover breakfast was a quiet affair, which mostly
consisted of a whining Anna at her distaste for the male
company the night before, but the girls eventually perked
up at around noon. The morning passed without incident
- we showered, and got ready for the all important races
that lay ahead. It soon became apparent that the dress
code was a cross between self-entitled and slutty.

I was feeling ambitious and slightly more confident after
the night before, or maybe it was just the alcohol still
running through my veins - whatever it was, I decided to
wear a peach backless dress, with a high collar neck that
closed at the back, and a slit up the side. My blonde hair,
with budding roots, fell in loose curls down my back,
silver heels completed the most elegant and fancy outfit I
had worn in what was almost two months. I even shaved
my legs.

July 15th, 2014
1.00pm

Blurry eyed, after my cat nap in the taxi I stopped for food in Galway. The scorching sun was blinding me and tearing my brain apart, still suffering with the alcohol from the previous night still in my system. We were pre drinking with a group of Jessica's friends who went to an all-boys private boarding school; coming from an all-girls private boarding school, the mixing of our two groups made sense. Very cliché.

It was when we were walking up the steps to the apartment that I first saw him. He was on the phone outside the front door with his elbow raised in the air so his cuffs were slightly pulled back to reveal what looked like a Rolex on his tanned arm.

He looked my way immediately, and I already felt violated by his glance. In a flush of embarrassment, I dropped my eyes at once. I stopped myself from stumbling up the steps as I passed him, and in the few seconds that it took for us to walk past him and into the building, I felt his clammy hand make its way down the gap of my backless dress and snap the tip of my thong. I glared up at him, only to see his curling grin staring down at me. His reaction was as if I had called his name and he'd looked up in involuntary response.

His teeth were the first thing I noticed. Two perfectly formed lips curtained his straight aligned teeth which were practically glistening, surrounded by stubble which contoured his prominent cheekbones. His chiseled face was sculpted so well that his entire face was thoroughly symmetrical framing his sleazy eyes, which had inevitably caught me staring in disgust. A combination of rage and confidence brewed inside me unexpectedly, and I strutted past him into the apartment after the girls, leaving my silky dress to brush against his knee.

I joined the girls and was introduced to an entire room of inquisitive strangers who knew everyone but me. Anna and Jessica were already friendly with this room of fresh out of school rugby jocks, and so I was more or less on the outside of this circle. I couldn't help but notice that they were all dressed close to identical to each other, the crowd of clones resembled a Ralph Lauren advertisement. All of the chinos and blazers and far too

expensive cuff links blurred into one big crowd of men.
People greeted me upon entry, I didn't know anyone's
names but I smiled and waved back at everyone. I was
surprisingly uncomfortable being ogled and undressed
with stares by a fresh crowd of old money snobs.

That brief sense of self confidence was destroyed in two
seconds flat with the slam of door as the tanned boy
from outside entered the room. He wasn't dressed like
the others I noticed, now that I had the chance to look at
him again without being obvious. His blazer was navy,
and his shirt white, rather than blue, and the chinos he
wore looked so different on him, perhaps because of his
slight frame they hung differently. He looked like he
went to Oxford or somewhere posh like that.

The girls and I took a table in the corner, and it was
obvious I was not the only one who had noticed this
Oxford boy who no one else seemed to know either.

"He saw me looking" Jessica was panicking "I haven't
seen him out with this group before though so maybe I
can still get with him."

"I don't see the attraction" I shrugged in response,
having not yet had the opportunity to disclose to them

what had happened upon our entry to the party.

"No I'm with Jessica on this one" Anna chimed in, "He's obviously gorgeous, but no one waste their time, I don't imagine any of the girls in here are good enough for him".

"Or he could just be horrible" I suggested.

The disappointment was evident on Jessica's face as she shrugged it off and changed the subject.

I couldn't stop myself from peeking occasionally through the screen of my hair at the horrible boy across the room. I could see his hand on his left leg was clenched into a fist, tendons standing out under his skin. He now had his blazer off and the long sleeves of his white shirt rolled up to his elbows, and his forearm was hard and muscular beneath his tanned skin. I made a mental note to not give him another thought, as I was sure that was what he wanted.

The pre drinks seemed to drag on longer and longer than these things usually did. I suspect my negative attitude and low expectations may have had something to do with this, but I was finding myself running out of ways to pass the time.

July 15th, 2014

03.00pm

After what seemed like an age, we split up into taxis to travel to the races and lost the group from the apartment. Between the three of us we made a few bets but no one was fortunate enough to actually win anything, so we collectively decided to spend the day at one of the outdoor bars as it was a rare occasion that the weather was this warm in Ireland. As the alcohol began to take affect, I became very aware of the fact that there were far more men than girls and I suddenly wished I hadn't worn such a skimpy dress. The four of us found ourselves outnumbered by a blur of beige chinos.

As I left the group and walked to the bar to get another drink, someone behind me muttered "Check out Miss 'don't touch my thong'" and I felt a sharp squeeze on my shoulder. I spun around and saw Oxford that had just been with our group, smirking while his hand was now sliding once again down my waist.

 "Nice dress."

I could feel the wrong kind of goose bumps emerging

down my spine.

I shrugged his sweaty hands off me and scanned the crowd for Jessica or Anna's familiar face.

He followed me along the bar.

"Now you won't find any fun looking over there. Why is it that you're ignoring me?" His advances continued but I zoned him out, my mind was growing foggier and all I was sure of was that he was relentless sin his petering and in his pursuit.

In an effort to avoid falling into the category of being a bitch, I sent him the message that I wasn't interested with a polite smile and proceeded to order my drink.

"So you're going to ignore me?"

His hand shoved my shoulder and I stumbled into a man standing with his back to me at the bar. I used this man, being the nearest person to me as a human shield and walked briskly away with a stranger in tow, my drink spilling onto my dress.

I heard a sinister laugh, followed by what was the awful English accent that I wished would go away.

"Do you not want the drink you left there?"

The tanned Oxford boy wasn't going to leave me alone. His voice was warm, possibly amused, but it was difficult to tell from his impassive expression. He looked mildly interested, but above all, intrusive.

"No its fine" I manage to blurt out eventually, and I thought I saw a ghost of a smile on his expression, but I wasn't too sure. Not wanting to make a scene in a room full of his kind, I started to walk towards the canopy area outside into the sun. I used my palm as a shield to block the sun as we looked out at the current race, I'm guessing he saw through my fake interest in horses.

"Did you bet? He persisted on forcing conversation out of me.

"Eerm no. Not the lucky type." I was being polite, while keeping an eye out for my friends.

"Nah me neither, not drunk enough yet" he joked. He was laughing slightly, but I felt he was laughing at me as way to assert his power over me, rather than at anything I had said. He launched into conversation, somehow feeling comfortable enough to confide in me about his father's problem with gambling, and how it had ruined his family, however my hangover combined with clear intoxication resulted in my lack of interest in listening. He fell silent, and I realized he had asked a question that I had not paid attention to. My cheeks heated at the realization, and I stood up straighter and squared my shoulders in an attempt to look taller and more intimidating. I glanced up at him. His smile was rueful, and he looked vaguely disappointed in my sudden lack of communication skills. He handed me a drink.

"An olive branch, to make up for the gin spill on your dress".

At that time, I didn't know better than to accept drinks from strangers.

"Should we go find the others?" I suggested in the hope that I could shake him off in the crowd and escape.

The girls were standing smoking against a bar table, and his friends were less than five feet away from them at another. As I walked towards our group of mutual friends, I could feel his gaze burning the back of my head as he followed me. I tried my best to strut with confidence over to the girls, as he made sure to fall behind - I was resenting my stupid backless dress. The glass began to feel cold and wet in my hand. I suddenly became aware of my feet trying to balance in my heels. When I reached girls, four boys had joined them. I grabbed what sounded like Jessica and leaned in to tell her I wasn't feeling well. I suddenly couldn't make out a single face. I tried to count my drinks to find the source of the problem. I heard voices muffling around me making some sort of commotion. The only thing I could focus my mind on was the overwhelming desire to go to sleep. I soon realized I was flailing around for anything comfortable to lean my head on so I could just have a few minutes of shut eye.

July 15th, 2014
????pm

Someone get her heels off.
I now couldn't tell if I was horizontal or vertical at this point. But the sensation of my shoes being removed suggested I was lying down.
She's had far too much to drink. I saw her just down three gins in a row.
Even in my obliterated state I could make out Oxford's

voice. That wasn't the truth either. He had handed me one gin, and I'd had one sip of it. I tried my utmost to protest, but only bile came out of my mouth.

Should somebody we get her an ambulance?

Yes, I thought. Somebody please, get me an ambulance.

No. I'll look after her and take her back and put her to bed.

July 16th, 2014

03.30am

I wasn't a freak, well I certainly didn't look like one. I was never self -conscious of my appearance. Not typically the centre of attention, but neither did I ever have a complaint.

My long blonde hair perfectly highlighted my baby blue eyes, and I myself was also tanned, tall, and thin. I was well aware that I wasn't ugly, and my confidence usually stemmed from that thought alone. But in the grey morning light I looked down at my body and suddenly it didn't look like mine. It was like an out of body experience.

I could make out that I was strewn across the couch in the apartment we had pre drinks in. My bare feet were crossed on the arm of the couch, my dress scrunched up around my waist. My previously snapped thong hung around my left ankle on full display. I didn't even know who had seen me like this, so I scrambled to fix myself before anyone else got the chance.

I was distracted from my self-examination, by the sound of voices in the adjacent kitchen. I turned my pounding head to see the source of the commotion, to see Oxford interlocked with a pretty brunette. My heartbeat has accelerated, and my cheeks were heating up again. Confused, I sourced my dead phone and gathered myself to make for an exit.

"We meet again" he prompted.

He was drunk now, pulling himself away from his friend. I was focusing 100% of my attention on not vomiting. His eyes were alight with some unknown thought. It took me a few seconds to find my voice.

"Thanks for taking me back. What happened?" I muttered.

He smiled, revealing the perfect white teeth I had noticed

earlier. He laughed smugly at my state. He really was condescending.

"Close the gate on your way out will you?" He was slurring his words.

I gathered he'd combined a little too many substances for one day. I slammed it firmly and marched down the drive. Thankfully, I didn't have to walk for long before I hailed a taxi and rattled off Jessica's address to the driver.

July 16th 2014

11am

I sat with Jessica's Mom in her front porch, drinking tea and rambling out false events from the night before, because in truth, there were too many blanks to fill. It didn't differ much from the truth, just without the passing out and losing the girls. I was too far gone to even feel guilty or judged. She was a gentle woman, and pretended not to notice my smudged make up and disoriented state. After an hour of awkward small talk, I excused myself to shower and make myself presentable for the day.

After my phone charged up, I discovered that Anna and Jessica had spent the night in the same apartment, I didn't even think to look for them when I left.

I decided I couldn't face going back there to get them, as I wasn't entirely sure of what happened to me the night before. I made the decision to take the early train back home and I would catch up with them during the week.

August 17th 2014
09.30am

I was sitting in my bedroom in Dublin, on the day I got my leaving cert results when I had my first flashback.

I stared down at the blood surrounding me, not sure whether the pounding in my head, or the pounding from my pelvis was causing me more distress and pain. I called out for Anna but she was long unconscious with a pizza slice in the next room. Was she in the room when this happened? My thoughts were slowly coming together enough for me to question where the blood

21

came from- had there been an accident, was it my blood, was it an unexpected period. It certainly felt like my blood, and I was certainly in pain, but I had not yet plucked up the courage to reach down and fully investigate. My thoughts were interrupted when the spinning room began to slow to a halt, and the door opened behind me and slammed shut. It was Oxford. My first thought was that he could help me, get me some tissue, get me some pain killers, or at least help me piece together what had happened. Someone had to know something. I grew frantic and called out for him to help but he quickly closed the door behind him and shushed me, stroked my head and cooed at me that I was okay, trying to convince me that it was all a bad dream and nothing had happened.

My voice began to quiver as I pointed out the blood and demanded an explanation- however his mind was elsewhere, he was hearing me but he wasn't listening. Instead, he just cradled me as my voice escalated to plain sobbing and rocked me whilst shushing me. In my distressed state I couldn't make out if he was attempting to comfort me or patronise me as if he knew what had happened. I could hear people gathering outside the door trying to get in, calling out for me, calling out for Anna and Jessica. It was as if he couldn't even hear them. His tanned arms tightly clutching me and rocking me slowly as if he were my mother and I were his injured child. My naive and fragile state chose to believe he was trying to help and I curled up into his arms, leaving a trail of blood on the sheets below us, and tried to cry myself to sleep.

The sharp pressing of his tongue invading my mouth awoke me, in conjunction with the hard pressing of his fists around my left breast. Startled and violated I attempted to wriggle out of his tight embrace, but to no successful. I mustered up whatever strength I could find and shoved him off.

"What happened to me?" I called after him, but I was met with silence.

I staggered to my feet and began to walk towards him
"I said what happened to me? Where is everyone else?"
Again, all I heard in response was running water, but this time with the addition of the bathroom door being slammed in my face.

I decided the notable aggression in his kiss was not drunken passion, but a clear indication of what might have happened.

My Mom calling me down for dinner pulled me out of my flashback. On my way downstairs, I sent a message to Jessica and Anna, hoping they would respond, but knowing they still wouldn't.

I sat through dinner with my Mom, with the realization for the first time of what had happened that night pervading my thoughts, and pretended nothing was unusual.

After dinner I went for a walk to allow myself to process my thoughts, and come to terms with what I thought had happened.

Instead I found myself thinking of my grandmother.

My grandmother died when I was twelve, younger maybe. I remember visiting her in the hospital in the last few days before her death and she made me smoke a drag of a cigarette. As obscene as it may seem, she had hoped that it would turn me off so much that I would never do it again so I wouldn't end up with lung cancer like her.

During her funeral my sister beside me cried. My mother comforted my father's bellowing cries. The entire church echoed together in sobs of mourning. But not me. I was so fascinated by the colours on the stained glass windows. I wondered why everyone wore black; I gazed around the room asking myself who all of the people were, I stared at the coffin trying to accept the fact that my grandmother lay inside there. I thought of her smoking, how disgusting the taste of the cigarette she made me try was, I wondered why she enjoyed it so much and how I'd promised her I'd never do it again. I wanted to ask her why she liked it, and I wanted to say goodbye to her. I really missed her, and I wanted to express this through the solidarity of tears. But I couldn't.

I thought about all the reasons that people cried.

It could be for a good reason, for a bad reason, for no reason, or just because they are emotional. When people cry, the usual reaction is to soothe them, to comfort them, in an attempt to make them feel better. However friendly this gesture may be, I can guarantee you that it almost never works. And it shouldn't. Crying is a way of the body trying to get rid of all emotional wounds through tears, and no matter what anyone says to you, it all must come out eventually. It's healthy. There's supposed to be no avoiding it. It's inevitable.

Except for me, in that moment, but I've never really questioned it. I've always assumed it just wasn't my way of dealing with things. But at that moment, as I was walking around in the rain, the realisation that I had been raped - I wished I could have cried. I wished I could have let my emotions get the better of me, and let my feelings go. I longed for the rain to wash away my tears, to ruin my mascara, for thick beads of black make-up stained tears to ruin the clarity of my porcelain skin. I wished my sobbing would resonate through the empty streets I was walking down- but they didn't.

I thought about the promise I made my grandmother never to poison my body as I inhaled deeply on a drag of my third cigarette.

Chapter two

August 22nd, 2014
4pm

I read somewhere that women release a hormone when sleeping with someone, the same 'love hormone' as when they are breastfeeding. Prior to the incident, I had slept with a few people, and was sure that I had never felt anything like that before, so I had a hard time believing it was true. What I was feeling then was far from any love hormone, and that feeling was lasting weeks.

I had fallen into the habit of showering, changing my clothes and repeating, multiple times per day. Despite the fact that it had been more than a month since I was last with him, but I could still smell his distinctive alcoholic scent, and I could vividly recall his touch against my skin, and the warmth of his clammy breath. I had never taken any kind of drug before that weekend either, except weed. I could still feel the sensation of the drugs taking affect, even though they had long left my system. As old fashioned as it may have seemed to my adventurous peers, the idea of putting yourself in danger like that just didn't appeal to me as a teenager. In fourth year in school our year head showed us a documentary of a girl in the UK who took a pill once at her 18th birthday and died straight away or something traumatizing like that. It was enough to put me off for life.

Neither of my best friends had engaged in a proper conversation with me since the races. They had dodged my calls, ignored my messages and made up excuses to not see me. In that weekend alone I had been date raped. I wondered if perhaps this was the reason for my friends to ignore me, and I attempted again to call Anna.

"Hello?"

She actually answered.

"Anna! What's up?" I didn't care that I sounded desperate at this point.

"Oh- em nothing. You turned off your caller ID."

"What happened? You've been avoiding me for weeks"

I heard her sigh at the other end of the line.

"Anna will you just be honest with me and tell me why

you're avoiding me."

After a brief silence she told me.

"Look, it's really nothing. It's just that, well, everyone knows that you slept with Ross and then disappeared. You didn't even text us, and everyone knows that he has a girlfriend."

I felt a ball of nerves gather in the pit of my tummy.

"Anna that's not true at all- why did you not ask me? You have no idea what really happened."

"Look its fine- its Jessica you should be speaking to about it. It's her friend."

I casted my mind back to a month previous, we all stood in a room and speculated about who he was, where he came from and about the fact that nobody knew him. Or his girlfriend.

"You don't even know him Anna."

Silence.

"…And if you asked me what happened or responded to my messages then you would know that"

Still silence. I couldn't tell if she felt bad or was still angry at me.

"Ok, fine. I don't know for sure what happened, I just

feel bad for his girlfriend."

"And what about your girlfriend Anna…"

I was angry that I had to guilt-trip my best friend for avoiding me for a few weeks and believing some stranger over me, but my need for a friend at that point was bigger than that.

"Look let's just go out this weekend and we'll talk about it then. Just us."

I agreed, half wondering why Jessica wasn't invited and half dreading telling them what happened.

August 24th, 2014

7.45pm

"….and then I found out that Andrew and Killian are both starting in my course and I only kissed Killian two weeks ago, how awkward?"

I was drifting in and out of listening to Anna going on and on about the drama I had missed. She very quickly forgot about Ross with the girlfriend that I had apparently scorned. I was baffled at how fickle she was, and how she had become caught up in such a disingenuous crowd- but a part of me was just grateful that she was past the stage of moaning for hours about her ex.

We walked along Rathmines road and turned into my local pub, flattered by the fact that we weren't asked for ID upon entrance. I headed straight for the bar while Anna went and looked for seats- I was relieved at how easily we had slipped back into our old routine. I knew that she had become a gin drinker from keeping up with her Instagram posts, so I opted for that to accompany the pint I was ordering. I found Anna out in the smoking area- I waded through the crowd, losing about a quarter of my pint along the way.

"You didn't tell me about your course anyway." She prompted, probably realising the entire walk to the pub consisted primarily of her talking about herself.

"Yeah, I have two weeks until I start. Drama."

"You just can't seem to stay away from the *Drama* can you?" she teased as she lit her cigarette.

I knew that she was referring to what happened after the races- we hadn't spoken about it yet. I gulped down my drink and decided I wasn't ready to dive into that just yet.

"Anyway Ms. Dramatic, what happened with that Ross guy anyway?"

It didn't matter if I was ready, she had decided that I was going to have that conversation.

"Ah just-" I choked on the mouthful of smoke she had just blown directly into my face.

I swallowed a ball of nerves and laughed.

"He just tried it on with me. I turned him down and fell asleep on the couch, I don't know what he told you but nothing happened and his girlfriend doesn't have anything to worry about."

She stared blankly at me, and I knew that she didn't believe a word of it, but she played along for the sake of not making things awkward.

"Okay, so *nothing happened*. I believe you" she lied.

August 24th, 2014
10.15pm

We had been chatting for a while now, after we quickly glossed over my little lie. I wondered how and why she had pretended to forgive me so quickly, after it had seemed to mean so much to her for the few weeks preceding our date. Her phone lit up on the table, with a string of notifications from a Whatsapp group that I wasn't a part of.

"So, it's getting a bit dead here" she suggested, gesturing around at the busy smoking area. "there's a house party in town I might head off to, if that's ok."

I knew that she was now finished with my company and wanted to move on to a better crowd. I didn't have a problem with that.

"Of course, I've probably had enough to drink anyway" I joked, glancing down at my untouched three quarters of a pint.

"I mean you could definitely come"

I tried to gauge whether this was a genuine invitation, as she had basically already excused herself from our date.

"Jessica will be there." She admitted after a long pause.

"You might get a chance to speak to her"

I agreed to go, with the intention to explain things to Jessica. I realized I now had to keep up with the lie I told Anna, or sit them both down and come clean.

August 24th, 2014

10.45pm

When we walked in, it was clear to me that we were the last to arrive. Dozens of sets of eyes turned their attention to us, sending a sudden rush of adrenaline through me, as I darted after Anna into the back room to 'put down my bag'. She immediately became flustered and started listing off names she had seen in the few seconds of our entrance, and I quickly realised that she wasn't interested in me or my plan to speak to Jessica. Just as I put down my bag, I turned around to offer her a drink, only to see the back of her red hair marching back out into the party.

I was left alone in someone's utility room at a random party where I didn't know anybody. I opened a can I found in someone's bag and started to walk out after Anna.

It took less than a second for Oxford to appear in the room beside me. His hair was wet, and he was dressed in an oversized hoodie- the same one he wore the morning after our encounter at the infamous races. He was silent,

34

and not drunk this time, and he came across almost nervous. The silence was broken by an awkward clearing of the throat on my behalf.

He came closer to my side of the cramped room and leaned towards me, and extended his hand to retrieve a bottle of vodka behind me. Obviously, this was the reason he had come in here in the first place and I was relieved that he had not come to personally greet me. My mind began to panic, he would leave, and I would have to walk out into the small crowd by myself, with even more judging eyes being thrown my way. My planning of an escape route was interrupted.

"So how are you?" His tone was teasing, and his smirk was clear on his blushing face as he kept his eyes on the floor.

"Not drunk enough" I suggested, as I took the vodka bottle from his grasp, and made for the exit into the room. Trying to act normally, I decided it would look better if I was the first to return to the party, rather than be seen to be following him around. However, my genius plan was put on hold, when my unwanted companion rejected my departure and pulled me back towards him, to lead me through the back door, to the garden, where a few people were smoking.

"Peer pressure" he prompted, as he nodded towards the scene in front of us, and rummaged in his pocket. I froze and stared at him.

"I don't , em," I began, I was cut off by someone signalling for me to share a lighter.

"I don't smoke" I blurted out, almost as a retaliation to my surroundings.

He pulled his empty hand out of his pocket, and waved it at me, implying that he didn't either. It wasn't exactly a lie, I didn't smoke. I didn't smoke tobacco anymore anyway.

It was standing outside in clouds of smoke, seeing his glaring eyes staring down at me that I realised that he wanted me again. Goosebumps appeared on the back of my neck and my whole body burned up with rage. I stomped back into the utility room.

"Why did you tell everyone we slept together?" I was straight to the point.

He laughed his horrible condescending laugh and leaned

back against the wall.

"Come again?"

My stomach turned at the sound of his voice. I had hoped I would never hear his condescending English accent again.

"You lied, we didn't sleep together. *You* slept with *me*. You raped me. " I felt pathetic when I heard the quivering in my voice.

"Are you talking about when you tried to have sex with me? At the races? Jesus, I had some explaining to do to Lauren. Cost me a girlfriend, you did."

His tongue traced the back of his teeth as he pulled the corners of his mouth into a sly grin. I couldn't believe he was actually trying to make me believe his lies. I was there.

"I was there." A confidence emerged from my anger. "I know that you put something in my drink and raped me."

He snatched the bottle from me and shoved me against the cupboard. My head smacked against the wood.

"You should be very careful about throwing around words like that. You wouldn't want to have people thinking you're crazy either."

His hand was pressing down on my chest. He brought his face right up to mine, his eyes inches from mine and stared into my soul. He lowered his voice.

"You got drunk, Ellen. You forced yourself on me and I stupidly gave in. What you did, caused Lauren break up with me. That is what happened, and no one will ever believe whatever lies you try and tell them."

He released me and stormed out of the room.

"My name is Ellie." I heard myself whimper.

August 25th, 2014

9.30am

Waking up in my own bed, I recalled finding Anna and making some excuse to leave soon after Oxford's ambush. Jessica had seen me leave and was now probably even angrier with me for not trying to patch things up with her. I found myself not caring. A surge of vomit rose from my tummy and I ran to the bathroom just in time to release it into the toilet. My Mom heard me retching and knocked on the door to ask if I was ok. I lied and turned on the shower to mask the sound of my

38

vomiting. The fact that I had a hangover from a few sips of one pint was pathetic, and that thought alone made me feel ten times worse about the night before.

August 26th, 2014
9.15am

My 'one-drink hangover' had appeared to last two days. I was once again awoken by the sudden need to be sick. While I was burying my head in the toilet, texts from Anna pinged on my phone, asking me to go to the gym with her.
I had no idea where this sudden interest in fitness had come from, but I felt it was in my best interest to keep her sweet.
After deciding to go, I walked to meet her and we walked the whole way back up Rathmines road towards the gym, chatting again like nothing had happened. I barely made it there without vomiting again, and I had to excuse myself twice to do so during our workout.

August 27th, 2014

9.15am

Yet again, like clockwork I was sick in the bathroom
under the guise of the water running in the shower. I
knew that three days of this meant that something was
wrong. Dialling the number of my family GP, I
rehearsed in my head what I was going to say.

*Hi, I've been sick for a few days in a row and I'm not
sure what's wrong.*

*Hi, I was drinking the other night, but my hangover has
lasted longer than usual.*

*Hi, I was raped a month ago and now I might have
morning sickness.*

I hung up the phone on the fourth dial tone before he
could answer.

August 27th, 2014

Noon.

On the bus to the other side of town, I kept my head

down. An old woman sat down beside me, and I felt a wave of shame wash over me, as if she knew where I was going.

Alighting a stop too early, I walked the rest of the way. The street sounds surrounding me were suddenly all very clear.

Children's laughter, the hum of the engines of unmoving cars stuck in a snake of traffic, the beeping of the pedestrian traffic lights waiting to go green, and the pounding of my heart against my chest.

The whizz of the automatic doors as I entered, the wheels of the trollies sliding along the dirty tiled floor, the slapping of groceries being thrown into shopping baskets, my footsteps walking through the aisles.

The fumbling of the small cardboard box as I picked it up, the rustling of the outer plastic layer as I scrunched it in my hand, the beeping of the scanner at the till, the judgmental grunt of the cashier, the zipper of my purse opening, the clanking of the coins as I counted them out onto the counter.

The rustling of the paper bag in my hand, the jostling of its contents, the "€2.75" of the bus driver, the ping of the bell to let him know where to let me back off.

The clicking of the key turning in the lock, the door banging off the wall as it swung open, my Mom chopping vegetables in the kitchen, the whistling of the kettle. My feet stomping up the stairs, the squeak of the bathroom door closing, the pounding in my ears, the tearing of the cardboard box opening, the sound of the plastic test hitting the tiled floor.

My nails scraping the floor and picking it up, the sound of my pee hitting the plastic, followed by a flush. A sharp intake of air, a deep sigh, and finally, silence.

August 27th, 2014

1pm

I stared at the two pink lines. I couldn't hear anything anymore, all of the sounds I was previously hyper aware of had now vanished. I went through the pile of packaging on the floor and read the instructions just to be sure. I was only fooling myself, there was no denying it. There was no escape.

I was disappointed in myself for briefly googling 'home

remedies' for this sort of thing on the dark web, but I knew deep down I'd never have the guts to pull off something like that. I knew I was in trouble but I didn't want to think about it any longer.

August 27th, 2014

5pm

After a long nap, I woke up hoping to have drummed up a solution to my problem. After some brief internet research, I discovered that I had to quickly come up with a large sum of money. With a grand total of €143 in my bank account, that was going to be difficult. The only person that came to mind was my half-brother, that would be willing to help me out, no questions asked. I sat there dreading the call I would have to make, thinking of stories that would sound believable. I was drawing a blank. There was only one other person I knew who had money to burn and was familiar with the UK. I rolled over and curled up under my white sheets and tried to force myself to go back asleep. I didn't want to be awake anymore.

Giving up, I rose and stood in front of my full length

mirror and took in what I saw.

My hair was tousled and tied up into a bun which was falling to the side. Lifting my jumper up over my head, I revealed my flat torso. As I turned to the side the light from my window caught my protruding hip bones and casted a long shadow across my pelvis. I was a size 6, my mid riff was almost concave and in a few short weeks this was going to be obvious- I was against the clock to deal with this problem.

Debating whether this was a problem or not was honestly a very short debacle in my head. I wish it did, but the thought of keeping it didn't remain in my mind for more than a few seconds. I couldn't go through with having a child at 18, let alone as a result of something so awful. I also didn't want anything to do with *him* anymore, let alone carry his child. Not when I knew I could never love it.

August 27th, 2014

7.45pm

I was successful in performing my charade of pretending I was fine at dinner – I was sure neither my mother or sister suspected anything was going on. I kept conversation light, excused myself and retreated to my bedroom.

There, the bright white screen of my laptop shone into my face as the only source of light in my room. I did everything I could to avoid it. I had opened Facebook and written 'Happy Birthday' to people I didn't even know, I put on my playlist, cleaned up my desktop, moved spam emails to the 'junk' folder, even read the induction information about college starting next month. After much procrastination, and I couldn't avoid it any longer, I searched up his name on Facebook and stared at his profile. Ross Cunningham- the name made me sick. I clicked on the message icon and began to type.

"Hi. We have a problem".

Chapter three

27th August, 2014

8.05pm

Ross is typing…

..

Ross is typing…

…

Ross is typing…

"And what's that?" was his curt reply.

Seeing his three attempts at a response, I was suddenly
aware that everything I typed would be on record, and
that anything I said could be screenshot and forwarded to
anyone. I didn't know him well enough to know if he
would keep our conversation private. I didn't actually
know him at all. I wasn't even sure if I wanted him
knowing anymore.

"Can I call you?"

..

..

Seen.

Knowing he probably wouldn't respond to that, I messaged again, deciding to take a different approach.

"Can we meet up? I have to talk to you about something."

The messenger icon instantly pinged in response.

"Sure, where will I meet you? I have my car so I can drive to wherever."

His eagerness indicated that he thought I was asking to hook up with him. Not wanting him to know where I lived, I suggested I start walking towards town and he could pick me up along the way.

"K."

After agreeing quickly, he arranged to meet me an hour later.

I threw on some old tracksuit bottoms that lay on my floor and loosely brushed through my tangled hair, spraying perfume around my aura to mask the smell of stale unwashed clothing and sleep.

Unable to think through what I was going to say, I took three swigs from a litre of vodka I had stashed under my bed for some courage. I threw on my big puffy coat and started walking towards town.

27th August, 2014
9.32pm

My ankles were damp from the splashes caused by cars driving through deep puddles at the side of the road. Despite the late August date, I could see the clouds of my breath every time I exhaled, and my cheeks were pink. Not knowing what kind of car to look out for, I stared aimlessly through my bloodshot eyes out into the traffic. A surge of panic pulsed through my body whenever a car came close to me. Every few minutes my trembling hand pulled out my phone to check for a message, and every time there was nothing.

I stopped to lean against the wall, and decided I would message him. Having been walking for over an hour I began to suspect that he wasn't coming. Just as I began to type, two white head lights appeared out of nowhere and blinded me. Squinting through the beams, I could make out his big lanky silhouette through the windshield, in the driver's seat. I put my phone back in my pocket, swung open the door and sat into the passenger seat beside him.

The car lurched forward and sped off down the road before I could say anything. Cautious that I might need an escape, I didn't put my seatbelt on. We drove in silence for a few minutes before he turned down a small dark lane and pulled in, switching the engine off, leaving the radio on.

My legs were like jelly and my whole body was trembling. I wasn't fearful, I was angry.

He didn't turn to face me when he spoke.

"What was it you wanted to ask me?"

"Tell you."

"Sorry?"

"Tell you. I had something to tell you."

He placed his hand on my leg, but before he could get any further I immediately slapped it away.

"That's not what I'm here for."

"You asked me to meet up?"

He sounded confused. He clearly thought this was a booty call. I was so angry that I didn't have time to be scared, fragile or offended. Slapping the palm of my hand against the radio dial, silencing the music, I turned to him and addressed him in a strong firm tone.

"I'm not going to talk about what happened. I'm going to talk about what is going to happen, Ross."

He stifled a smug laugh.

"I'm pregnant. I'm pregnant and I haven't had sex with anyone. I'm pregnant because of what you did to me at the races."

"I didn't touch you." He voice was raised.

"Yes you did, I'm not getting into that. You know you did. I need the money to sort it out."

"I'm not giving you shit."

"Then I'll have the kid and demand money from you every month until it's eighteen."

"It's not mine."

"It's not fucking anyone's." I snapped "It's not even going to get the chance to be a real thing. You need to give me the money to make sure of that."

For some reason I felt like my dad when he was trying to convince someone to close a business deal. There was no emotion in my voice, I was matter of fact and straight to the point. There was no room to be weak, I was determined to leave with the promise of the money.

He took out a small orange box and started to roll a cigarette between his clammy tanned fingers. When he had finished licking the paper, I took it out of his hand, put it between my lips, pulled out a red lighter and lit it.

"I thought you didn't smoke." he scoffed at me.

"Don't fucking chastise to me. Don't talk to me."

He began rolling another cigarette for himself. He rolled down his window and took a long deep drag before exhaling out into the dark lane.

"You said you didn't smoke either." I snapped back at him.

"I thought I wasn't allowed talk to you"

"You're fucking not."

"Okay then."

We sat in silence and angrily stared out through the windscreen into the darkness, inhaling and exhaling until we each just had dirty brown filters between our fingers. When we I was finished I threw mine in his face.

"I'll need about 900 pounds, flights, and somewhere to stay. I can sort out the latter, it's the money I need from you."

I didn't look at him but I could feel him staring at me. I heard him swallow.

"Fine. I'll transfer it by the end of the week."

I didn't respond or look at him. A part of me was angry that he had just admitted what he had done so easily like that, like it was nothing. I clicked the door to unlock it, stepped out and slammed the door behind me. I heard the window roll down, and his stupid English accent calling after me.

"Aw, Ellen come on I'll drop you home. Don't be daft."

I knew that he had seen my name on Facebook earlier that day from my message.

I bent down into the window frame, and for the first time that night stared at him directly in the face. I could see his confused eyes had tears in them. His hand was stretched over the steering wheel, the other arm resting on the clutch.

He wasn't smiling, but he had that stupid smug look on his face again. I couldn't find it anywhere in me to feel any kind of pity for him. I corrected him for the second time.

"It's Ellie."

29th August, 2014
4pm

I still hadn't heard from him. The night I met him, as soon as I got home I had sent on my bank details and waited for the money to come through. To be honest, I had told him a white lie. I didn't have enough money for flights or anywhere to stay- I needed him to help with all of it, but thought that if I asked for that much that it I would have been far less likely to get anything.
I had no idea how much money he or his family had, I had judged his wealth entirely from his appearance and his overall demeanour. I began to panic, and started loosely looking at other options, in case his promise fell through and the money didn't materialise.

1st September 2014

10.30am

Growing worried by his lack of contact, I opened my chat with him and thought about sending yet another message.

There was a stack of unanswered messages staring back at me. He had blocked my phone number so I couldn't call him, which was not looking good for me. I didn't care that he thought I looked desperate. At this point I didn't care if he told anyone, I just wanted the money before the situation could progress any further. I knew deep down that a part of me just wanted it done before I could change my mind.

Accepting the fact that I wouldn't get the money from him, I thought of other ways that I could drum up 900 pounds. I came to the conclusion that I had to turn to someone else to ask for money- but this would only ever be a loan, I would have to pay it back. This wasn't their fault.

I texted my older brother and created up a semi credible lie. I sent a generic conversation opener, and was met with an incoming Facetime call. I declined.

I texted quickly making an excuse about having poor connection and told him I had a small favour to ask.

"I need to borrow some money, but I promise I'll have it back to you in the next few weeks. I'll pay back a certain amount every week. I can work it out."

A few short minutes past before his response.

"How much are we talking? And what is it for?"

I wanted to keep it vague.

"I'd rather not say to be honest, - as much as you can. I need about a grand before the end of the week."

My phone immediately rang.

"What do you mean you need it for the end of the week? What the hell is going on?"

"I just... I'm in some trouble ok and I really need it. "

"You involved with some sort of fucking gang Ellie? Did you tell your Mom?"

"No. And please don't tell Dad either. Please, I just really need this money."

"Is this for some sort of dumb girls trip or something

because I am not paying for that."

"No I swear it's not, I'm just really stuck. Don't tell Dad, please."

"Oh I know." He laughed. My heart was pounding, how could he know?

"Dad's finally making you pay your own car insurance isn't he? Ha. He didn't do that to me until I was 21."

I sighed a sigh of relief and forced a fake laugh.

"Alright fine, you got me. But I promise I'll pay it back to you. I just don't want to lose my car right before college starts."

He agreed. The diligent accountant that he was, he drew up a payment plan for me. I had to pay back 115 every week for 9 weeks. He wouldn't do it if he couldn't make any kind of profit from interest on the loan.

I panicked about how I couldn't pay that back myself, but knew that it bought me some time to pester Ross for the money he promised.

As soon as I hung up the phone, I went straight into problem solving mode.

In my research, I saw that there was one private clinic in Belfast who could offer pregnancy termination services.

Train tickets up north were significantly cheaper than flights to England, and not being more than two hours away on a train somehow felt like less of a big deal than leaving the island. Before I could mentally talk myself out of it, I scheduled a consultation and booked a train ticket to go up the following weekend.

1st September 2014
11am

I was back on a train again. I sat in the same kind of seat I had done when I was going to the races with Anna- third booth on the left, right up against the window. I hadn't heard from her in a few weeks. In the days after the party I had declined her calls, made excuses not to see her and left her messages unread. The last time I had seen her, was when I had vomited twice.
We were in the gym, I excused myself to the toilet and projectile vomited onto the front of a cubicle door. Having followed me in, she saw my mess and laughed at what she assumed was a hangover. She had no idea what it meant or where I currently was.

57

I felt awful for not trying to patch things up with Anna either, but I was mostly disappointed that she had decided to side with people that she barely knew against me.

As I watched the scene outside the window gradually change from the concrete grey buildings of the city, to open greens fields, I wondered if most female friendships had fickle, bitchy undertones, or if I had just been unlucky. The three of us had been friends for years in school, but it had only been that Summer when we graduated that they had started to show their true colours. It seemed that as soon as they weren't forced to see me every day in class, their loyalty soon began to lie elsewhere.

1st September 2014

2pm

The lady at reception was really nice. She took my (fake) name and details, and lead me to a clean waiting room with purple chairs. I sat there, digging my nail into the side of my thumb, sick with nerves.

"Aisling O'Reilly?"

A young girl quickly rose, and scurried off after the nurse that called her name, her Mom following quickly behind her.

"Mom, you can come in if you have Aisling's permission."

They went in together.

"Grainne Smyth?"

A couple in their mid-twenties got up and walked hand in hand after the nurse a few minutes later. I was the last one left.

"Ellen?"

I almost forgot my fake name, and took a few seconds to register that I had only given one name. I had panicked and thought of the last name that stayed in my brain.

"Ellen..?"

"That's me"

I traipsed after her, stumbling over my doc martens on my way up.

"Ok so, Ellen. Is it just Ellen?"

I gave her a look.

"Yep. Just Ellen."

"Ok, *Ellen*. What do you need today"

I made up a story, but I got the general point across. She didn't really pretend to listen to the details, she just took down the medical information she needed on her clipboard.

"Ok. So you're in the lucky position of having discovered this at a very early stage. You are eligible for the option of a pill. You'll need to take one, and come back the next day and take a second one. It's very simple- it's quite cheap and you will only be sick for about two days."

This would have sounded perfect, if I was able to get away with being in Belfast for two days in a row, which I knew I wouldn't.

"Is there any other way I could do it? Is there an option to do it in one day?"

I guess from the sympathetic look on her face that she understood the issue from my south Dublin accent.

"We can offer a D&C procedure" she explained as she whipped out a leaflet.

"This doesn't technically terminate a pregnancy, but clears out the womb and cervix area completely. It simply removes the contents, a little bit like a hoover."
I grimaced.
"And I can get that in one day?"
"Yes but this is a medical procedure. You will be put asleep under general anaesthetic and have to stay here until you are fit to go home, which could take a few hours, but it will all be in one day. It also costs around 600 pounds. A little bit more for euro."
I mulled it over.
"You don't have to make a decision today. You just have to sign a form here four working days before you come to have it done. There is a counselling service here that we offer if you require any help with your decision and if you need to speak to someone afterwards."
She was very matter of fact about the whole thing, grabbing pamphlets and leaflets from every which way in an effort to hurry me out. I stopped her.
"I'll do it. Can I sign the form? For a procedure four days from now."
She stopped.

"You can take as much time as you-"

"No. I want to sign it. Can I pay when I come to have it done?"

She put down the leaflet in front of me and walked over to the door.

"Let me just get the forms now."

She riffled through her filing cabinet for some forms, and placed them down in front of me. She pulled up some images on her iPad and demonstrated exactly what would happen. I zoned out, not wanting to think about the exact medical details of what was going to happen. I didn't take science in school so it was all looking very foreign to me. If I am honest, I was glad that I didn't fully understand what I was signing up to.

1st September, 2014

5pm

On the train home, I decided to reach out to Anna. I wasn't going to tell her about anything, but I felt that even speaking to her about anything might make me feel better. I also didn't want her to suspect anything. I pulled out my phone to text her, and saw a message from an unknown number on my screen.

"What's it like?"

I clicked into it. The number wasn't saved and I didn't recognise it. I saved the number to my phone, and went to check the contact photo that was attached to it. I opened Whatsapp, and opened a chat, as if to send him a message. A small circle in the top corner appeared and I clicked on to the image. Three of the clones in chinos and blazers smiled back at me, all with the same sunglasses on, all holding pints. I typed back.

"What is what like? Who is this?"

I didn't know what they were talking about, or what they wanted. I suspected that Ross had maybe spoken to one of his friends about what happened, and maybe they were reaching out so that he could apologise or find out more. I wasn't sure. Another message came through.

"What's it like to be a slut?"

I blocked the number before they could write anything else.

I typed into my Whatsapp group with Jessica and Anna.

"Anyone around for a chat this evening?"

I wanted to tell them what happened. Both of them, even Jessica. Anna quickly started typing.

"Not tonight! Sorry."

Jessica never responded.

5th September 2014

7.45am

If she asked, I would tell my mom that college started a day earlier than it did. I only took a small handbag so that no one would suspect anything. I didn't take my car, I booked a taxi to bring me to the train for 8am. I took my gym clothes and a water bottle in case my Mom wondered why I was gone so early. I had everything planned out.

My train left from Connolly station at 8.30am and arrived at 10.40am, just over two hours before my appointment. I remembered the way to the clinic and I was feeling anxious and apprehensive about being there. As I walked the streets of Belfast, I felt as though every single person that passed me knew exactly what I was doing there. Every woman with a child, every man that caught my eye, they all knew.

I followed google maps on my phone to be sure, and turned the corner to where the clinic was. I was thankful that I had my headphones on.

A small crowd of angry women were shouting something at me as I approached the doors. I kept my head down and looked at my feet, so that I wouldn't read their lips to see what they were shouting. I had read that sometimes people who didn't agree with this kind of thing appeared outside clinics to guilt people into changing their mind. However, they hadn't been there last time so I thought that I was safe. Regrettably, I lifted my eyes twice and saw signs with graphic pictures of massacred babies and bloody handprints. I thought of my own massacred body and the blood on my hands. If I hadn't been so determined to be rid of the reminder of being raped, I probably would have turned around and gone straight home. I opted to ignore them. I turned up my music and walked straight in.

As I sat in the familiar waiting room, I tried my best to clear the images I had just seen from my head. Opening my mobile banking app, I refreshed the screen three times to be sure that my brother's loan had come through. Thankfully, it had.

I heard my fake name being called once again, this time I was prepared for it, and I followed the nurse to a different room this time.

I had never had a general anaesthetic before, so I had to stop my legs from shaking with nerves as I changed from my clothes into a mint green gown.

Once I lay back, a small needle was put into the back of my hand, and the nurse started to slowly count back from ten. I stared up at the grey square tiles on the ceiling and counted with her.

5th September 2014
1pm

My heart slow heartbeat was the only sound I could hear when I could feel myself beginning to come round again. My slow breathing began to increase and I eventually opened my eyes.

I didn't think to let myself feel any physical pain, the only thing I felt was a huge relief that this whole chapter was over, I could forget about it, and go back to normal.

I sat for a few hours in the same room, before I was given the all clear that I could leave. In that time, I did nothing but stare at the walls. I didn't turn on my phone, I didn't think about what had just happened, I just sat and existed. I wasn't allowed to drive for the next few hours, so I had to have proof that I was getting a lift from the clinic in order to be discharged. Thankfully my taxi driver didn't have a problem with coming inside to claim me.

I was thankful that I had someone to walk out past the protestors with, even if he was a complete stranger who didn't speak much English.

5th September 2014
8pm

I was back at the train station, and I felt as though nothing had happened. My phone was still powered off, and I had no desire to turn it on to see if anyone had bothered to ask where I was, or noticed I was gone. I wanted to be alone with myself. I didn't want to think about paying back the loan to my brother, or pestering my rapist for the money he promised, or about the text I had received from a stranger, or how I had begun to grow apart from my friends. I was starting college the following day, so I dedicated the time it took to wait for the train to thinking about that.

Drama. I was almost certain that no one from school, or from the boys' school would be doing it. I thought about my audition, and the people I had met there, and wondered if they had all been offered a place too. It was nice to have something positive to focus my attention on, so I could ignore my reality for a little longer.

The train pulled up and screeched to a halt. Nobody came out from the doors I was waiting in front of, so I pushed the button and walked on alone.

5th September 2014

11.30pm

I made it home without incident. When I was finally back in my own bed, I switched my phone on. I had fourteen missed calls from my Mom and an abundance of worried messages from her. There were four messages from my brother, checking with me if the money had gone through, and three more messages from new numbers that I didn't recognise.

I went into my Mom's room and woke her to let her know I was home. I apologised for not letting her know I was spending the day at the gym and getting some last minute things ready for college. She was too tired to think about the logistics of it, or suspect that I wasn't telling her the truth.

Back in my room, without properly reading the string of random messages, after seeing the words 'Slut', 'Whore', 'Ross' and 'Liar'; I blocked three more numbers before closing my eyes for the night.

Chapter 4

September 6th, 2014
6.45am

I eventually began to feel something the following morning when I woke up in my own room. It was only then that the impact of what had happened the day before fully hit me. In the absence of any physical pain, a heavy weight pushed down on my chest, preventing me from getting up. I struggled to keep my eyes open for more than a few seconds. I rolled over, to go back to sleep, and it took hitting the snooze button on my alarm clock five more times until I actually woke up.

After mentally prepping myself for a few minutes, I sat up, swung my legs over the edge of my bed and stared down at my chipped nail polish on my toes. I watched as a single tear splashed down onto my thigh and slowly dripped off the side of my leg onto the sheets. Another tear followed suit, this time landing just above my knee. It didn't take long until they became more frequent until I couldn't avoid addressing them any longer. With a sharp exhale that puffed my cheeks out, I pulled myself up and walked over to my mirror to see the damage. My eyes were puffy and red, my nose dripping, and the remnants of yesterday's mascara had created a blurry outline around my bloodshot eyes. Relocating to the bathroom, I used the familiar disguise of the sound of the shower to mask the sounds of my sobs rather than my retches this time.

After a brief cold shower, I went into my room to try to make myself presentable. In a feeble attempt, I pulled my hair into a loose plait, and bent the smudge of eyeliner into shape with my thumb. I shook myself, gathered my bag and books, and went downstairs to face my mother.

"Oh honey, have you been crying?"

My disguise hadn't helped at all.

"Yeah, I'm just a bit nervous for today."

"Well you can't go out looking like that , sit down here." She flapped her arms in the direction of the chair in front of her, gesturing for me to sit and let her tweak my appearance. I would normally have recoiled at the thought of my mother having any involvement in fixing me, but that morning I let her. I watched as she ran up the stairs to get the equipment she needed. She was in her element. I let her shake out my wet plait, and brush through the tangles. She ran the hairdryer over the ends and twisted the thick strands around her curling tongs, so my hair would hang in loose curls. A wave of guilt ran through me that worsened with every stroke of her fingers through my hair. She had no idea what was going on in my mind and her efforts to cheer me up were so pure and I could see that they came from such an innocent place. It would kill her if she knew. I stopped her, when she tried to add her make up to the makeover. I could tolerate and was glad of her fixing my hair, put poking around at my face with her make up brushes was more than I could handle. I left far earlier than I needed to.

September 6th, 2014
8.30am

I sat outside my new college and waited for the doors to open. I pulled out my yellow box of cigarettes and started rolling. I smoked outside for a few minutes before following a small crowd of people inside the building. I had wasted half an hour watching the early morning traffic go by, fiddling with my cigarette, that I hadn't noticed that the porter had come out and the doors had been opened.

We were led into a large room with tiered seating, like a cinema, only at the top there was a whiteboard instead of a screen. Sitting at the back on my own, I sat through the induction. This involved listening to preppy, annoying current students give their accounts of what was in store for the next four years. I followed a schedule I was handed and traipsed around to three classroom- based lectures, hovering at the back, pretending to listen to different tutors outline what we would be covering through-out the semester. I couldn't focus on a single word any of them said, and I watched everyone else frantically scribble down notes, as I hummed idly and clicked my pen. At the end of the last class, I stared down at my blank notebook and waited until the end to leave. I watched as crowds of my fellow students began to strike up conversation with each other, break off into different groups, and all head off in different directions together.

Looking for a way to seem busy, I checked my phone, to only see a message from my mom. When I thought I was the last person left in the room, I eventually rose and gathered my bag to leave.

A dark red patch on the blue plastic chair below me caught my eye, and I immediately sat down. As I started to panic, my mind began racing. I had no idea what the procedure meant for my period, and I wasn't sure whether this stain was from my period, or bleeding as a result of what happened. I didn't know if that was normal or not.

I felt something hit my back. I turned around to see a dark blue hoodie on the back of my chair that didn't belong to me. I grabbed it and looked up.

"Looks like its shark week." An animated, effeminate voice laughed at me.

My cheeks flushed pink and I laughed straight back.

"You'd think I would have been more prepared for this by now." I signalled to the hoodie and raised an eyebrow.

"Use it to tie around your waist until you can sort yourself out. Come on."

He flailed his hysterical camp arms around the air, signalling for me to follow him out of the room. I tied the hoodie around my waist and did as I was told.

We walked down the long corridor into the girls' bathroom. I couldn't help myself from giggling at his confident, camp strut into the wrong toilet.

He shut down a few judging stares from a group of girls by shooing them away with his camp hand gestures, the rings on each finger jingling as he did so. I went into the cubicle to assess the damage.

I looked down and saw that I was saturated with blood, it had managed to get through my pants and had stained both the inside and outside of my leggings. I used my emergency pad in my bag to rectify the damage for the moment.

"Can I bring this back in for you tomorrow?"

I stepped out of the cubicle, pulling the hoodie over my head. It covered my knees. I looked up at him and took him in.

He was well over 6 foot 5, and was wearing a tight black mesh long sleeved top, which revealed an outline of his silver nipple rings. He lifted his eyes from his phone and looked me up and down, sniggering at the oversized hoodie dwarfing my frame.

"Well aren't you a nymph. Of course. Smoke?"

September 6th, 2014

4 pm

I watched him roll himself a cigarette between his skinny fingers, as I walked beside him through the building, off the grounds of the campus and towards town. His legs were so long that for every one stride he took, I had to take two. I scurried along beside him. He stopped.

"I have to take a picture of this."

He took out his android and snapped a picture of an old turquoise bike with a pretty basket of flowers in the front propped up against a lamp post.

"Get on it."

He signalled for me to hop on the saddle, and I did so, posing for the camera. The bike detached from the pole, as there was no lock or chain keeping it attached.

"It's not locked" he suggested

"You can't take it" I snapped back, not sure if he was serious or joking.

He rolled his eyes.

"I won't take it. We'll just borrow it." He pushed my body forwards and sat on the saddle behind me. I laughed at his bravery and gave in.

"Ok, five minutes."

He pedalled with his long lanky legs and wrapped his bony arms around my waist. I sat on the crossbar and attempted to steer the handlebars. It was extremely painful, but I was too embarrassed to let him know. We weaved around the traffic as drivers beeped and shouted profanities at us, which only made us more animated and spurred us on. I noticed some tattoos on his hands and I made a mental note to examine them later. We made it about twenty feet before the bike collapsed to the floor, taking us both with it, sending the flowers flying.

"See?" I managed to shout at him through panicked giggles as I scrabbled for the flowers.

"Shark week is back!" He shouted in hysterics as he pointed at the blood seeping through my leggings, this time from my scraped knees. Crawling over to me he

77

acted out an exaggerated charade of giving me a big kiss on my wound to make it better. He sent me into the off license while he walked the bike back to where we had borrowed it from, keeping his promise of returning it. After our brief brush with theft, we sat at the canal with a six pack of Heineken between us, and I listened as he told me all about the tattoos I had noticed earlier.

"This one is a thermometer." He traced the bottom of his ankle. The blue ink was now faded and the red lines were blurred.

"What does it mean?"

"Nothing, I just thought it looked cool." He chortled an infectious laugh and his natural smile revealed his crooked teeth.

"Well I think it still does." I smiled back.

His hands were illustrated with beautiful images, symbols and words. He talked me through them but glossed over their meaning. If they were significant, he wasn't going to share.

"Do you have any tattoos?" he turned the conversation over to me.

I laughed. "God no, I'm far too scared of needles for that."

He scoffed at my comment. "We'll see about that."

Time passed and the sun began to set on our first day at college. I learned his name was Rónán, but he preferred to be called Ró. He had taken a year out before going to college and so he was a year older than I was. He had spent that time travelling and discovered his love of drama through participating in an acting workshop in Madrid, despite not understanding a word of Spanish. He worked part-time as a hairdresser and claimed that he wanted nothing more than to chop off my long golden hair and bleach it into a platinum bob. I politely declined. Thankfully, he also managed to tell me about everything we were supposed to have learned about the course that day and took pictures of his notes to send to me.

After we went our separate ways, and I was walking home, I realised that I didn't look at my phone for the entire time we were there and I had actually managed to distract myself from everything that had gone on before.

Conscious that this charade was too good to be true, I made the mistake of checking my phone. I was met with a notification that alerted me to the fact that I had been added to a Whatsapp group with numbers I didn't recognise, but also one that I did- Jessica's. I scrolled through the messages.

Poor Ross honestly, disgusting what people will do for attention.

Another one.

I took history with her and I just knew that something was off about her.

Another one.

Why would someone with as much money as her try to scam Ross out of a grand? Don't get it.

I scrolled, another one.

She's a slut, what did you all expect.

And then I saw the message that hurt the most.

She told me that she may as well just scam some money off him now, seeing as she was getting so much shit for breaking them up already. From Jessica.

I scrolled through the rest of the messages, but they all had the same sentiment. Most of them were numbers I didn't recognise, but this time I didn't bother to check whose pictures were attached. I had noticed some of them were from girls I was at school with and was never really close to, but I was bitterly disappointed with Jessica's message, and I couldn't get the vile words she had written out of my head the whole way home.

September 10th, 2014
7.30pm

Ró led me up the steps of a secluded car park in Temple Bar, shushing me as I complained that my shorter legs were beginning to feel sore. The clinking bottles of wine grew heavier in my hands with every step.
"How much longer? We've easily walked up ten flights."
"Sorry, I forgot that it must be difficult for a nymph." He winked at me as he twirled on the landing at the top and pushed through a thick red door. I was beginning to get used to his constant sassy tone. Later I would learn that this was how he showed platonic affection.

"Here we are, nymph. Some wine, please." He grabbed the €7 bottle from me and unscrewed the cap, pouring the contents directly into his mouth. I walked after him through the doors and took in the view.

The twinkling lights of what felt like the whole city sparkled up at me, the sounds of engines and beeping below us muffled into background noise. He grabbed my hand. "This part is dangerous alright?" He guided me onto the ledge. It appeared that we were not quite at the top of the building yet. I looked down.

"No, Ró I'll just fall. I'll wait here."

"You didn't get this far to chicken out. Come on." He gently coaxed me along the edge of the ledge and stopped at a rusty old ladder. "Now climb the steps and wait at the top."

I followed his instruction and tried to avoid looking down and ignore my trebling limbs. I felt my knees buckle as I shuffled along the ledge, whispering to myself not to look down, as every time I did, I felt my stomach drop. My clunky boots made the manoeuvre more difficult than it needed to be.

Once I had made it to the top, I sat on the roof of the car park and waited for him to join me. He didn't take long.

"Now" he panted, once he reached me, "the wine."

"Thank you very much", I sang back at him, and gulped down three mouthfuls to extinguish my fear of heights. I passed it back to him.

"How did you discover this place?" I asked, curious as to how he managed to find such a pretty view of Dublin.

"Isn't it romantic?" he prompted. "One day we will both sit here with our beaus, and we'll look back at how terrified you were to even join me."

I laughed. "I don't think I'll have a *beau* any time soon." I mimicked. "Besides, we'd definitely need more than two bottles of wine for that." I snatched the bottle back from him and took another swig.

"Come on then, tell me who's turned you off men."

I looked down at my legs dangling over the city and thought about how easily I could jump. A combination of the wine, the adrenaline from our dangerous ascent, and the subject of men caused a lump to gather in my throat, and tears to well up in my eyes. He saw me.

"Aw god Ellie lets not make this a pathetic pity party."
He teased. I knew that he was trying to make me laugh.
"Chin up, come on. Don't talk about it if you don't want
to. He isn't worth it, and whoever he is, he'll never make
it up here with you to see this romantic view." I smiled.
After staring out across Dublin below us in silence for a
few minutes, I eventually wiped my eyes and nose and
cleared my throat. I drank more wine. I filled the silence.
"You never answered my question." I nagged
"What's that? "
"How did you find this place? It's a pretty secluded
place."
He smiled and looked down at his dangling brogues. He
cleared his throat.
"Actually an ex brought me up here once." He seemed
embarrassed after his 'men are trash' speech to admit
that he had been here with an ex- boyfriend.
 "Oh really?" I laughed as he began to blush. "Well was
he at least nice?"
His mouth curled into a smirk as he stifled a bashful
laugh. I took another gulp from the bottle. He rolled his
eyes at me

"She."

I spat out my wine, spraying the contents out over the side of the building, drenching the oblivious pedestrians below.

Chapter 5

September 10th, 2014

8.10pm

"I'm so sorry." I mumbled, "I just assumed.."

"Assumed that I was into guys?" he interrupted me.

"Yeah I'm so sorry that was really ignorant of me."

"Bold of you to assume I'm not "

I smiled sheepishly at him and then looked at the floor. I didn't want him to see my confusion.

 "I'm sorry."

He didn't go on to define his sexuality to me, and it didn't come up much again.

October 4th, 2014

9pm

I sat upright in a black swivel chair and stared at myself in the mirror. My left leg was bouncing quickly with nerves, as I could see Ró in the reflection behind me measuring out six inches of my hair with a comb and hold it up. My stomach dropped when I saw how much six inches really was.

"Less" I snapped

With an eye roll and a click of his tongue, he moved his fingers down and held it up again.

"This is as low as I'm going. Final offer."

It still looked much more than I wanted. Letting out a huge sigh, I closed my eyes and gave in.

"Alright fine, do it before I change my mind."

I squinted my eyes shut as he sprayed my hair until it was wet, and combed through it. He wasn't very gentle and I felt the comb pulling as it broke through every tangle in my long mane.

I covered my face with my hands as I heard him snipping away and felt the wet clumps of hair fall away down my back and onto the floor. Opening my eyes, I could see through the gaps on my fingers, the large clumps of golden curls landing in a large pile on the floor around my feet.

"Okay. You can look now."

Lifting my head, I pulled my hands away and looked up at the results. My long golden locks were gone, my hair now hung so it barely met my shoulders. My dark honey roots were now the colour of all my hair. I was very plain without my hair. I barely recognised myself.

"Ew." I said "did my face always look like that?"

"Oh I'm not finished sweetie." He pulled out a small pink pot of peroxide and poured it into a mixing bowl. "It's happening."

The peroxide burned my scalp as he lathered it on. He didn't split it into sections or use a brush- just loaded it all on as if it were shampoo. He then covered my entire head in a plastic sheet.

"Now sit for me for 25" he picked up his keys. "I'm heading out for more supplies. Keep yourself entertained."

I heard the door close behind him and itched at my burning head. A lump of bleach gathered on my fingernail and I wiped it on his black gown when it began to sting. I spun the chair around and looked around his room. Piles of cheap hair products stacked up against his shelves, and there were a few mirrors against the walls. The only other furniture in the room were two black swivel chairs beside a sink in the corner, and a mattress on the floor, with dark red velvet sheets.

My phone pinged. There was a notification from some-one called Dan on Facebook. I opened it.

A video played of a group of girls from school all laughing and joking. The camera was shaky but I could make out Jessica's face among the crowd. They were all walking towards my house, making obscene gestures as they went along. When they reached my house they took out a white marker and drew messy illustrations of phallic imagery on the back of my car, along with the word 'slut'.

After seeing this, I sat my trembling body back in the chair and thought carefully about what to do. I wouldn't let myself cry, and I had to block the thought of seeking revenge out of my head to stop myself from actually doing it. I clicked out of the video and went onto investigate Dan's profile. I could see from his page that he was dating Jessica. They stared back at me smiling in a photo, Jessica dressed in a blue dress and Dan in a suit-his arm was tight around her waist. One hundred and fifty-three people liked the photo. After blocking him, I ran out of Ró's ground floor apartment, with bleach in my hair and a plastic gloopy hat on. For the first time, I saw the vandalism on the back of my car which I hadn't noticed before, and I was heartbroken at the fact that I had driven across town with those words written on the back. Wondering how many people had seen it, I frantically wiped at the marker with my hands until they hurt. The marker didn't move. Tears began to well up in my eyes as I panicked about Ró seeing this and me having to explain my dirty secret to him.

October 4th, 2014
9.25pm

Sitting with Ró in his driveway, we silently wiped the rubbing alcohol along the boot of my car. Thankfully, the marker was giving way.
"It's those kids down at 16b, I know it" he was furious.
"They're always down at this end of the road with their bikes."
I couldn't bring myself to tell him the truth.

"It's fine" I laughed so he wouldn't question the tears
gathering in my eyes. "It's coming off anyway."
An alarm on his phone went off, and his eyes lit up. He
quickly forgot about the car.
"Yes! Its shampooing time."

I sat back in the chair in his room, so my head draped
over his sink and closed my eyes as he gently scrubbed
at my scalp, humming while doing so. I tried to block
out the thoughts of what they had done to my car. On my
eighteenth birthday, Jessica and I had driven around
Dublin in my brand new car for hours. The excitement of
something so new and grown-up masked the mundane
rainy afternoon. Now she was showing up at my house at
night with strangers to deface the same car. I was sure
her sunglasses were still on the back seat.
Once Ró was finished, he blow-dried my new hair into a
straight, slightly grown out bob.
I looked at myself and actually felt better. Despite my
expectations, I actually preferred this hair for me. I
didn't look as innocent and breakable as I did with long
golden curls. I swivelled round. He was staring at me,

with his hands clenched together, his face beaming with pride.

"Ró? Can I tell you something?"

I told him what happened. I told him about going down to the races, about what Ross did to me, about what I went through alone, and about the messages I had been receiving.

After a long silence, he cleared his throat. "So the day we met, you…" he pointed at my crotch.

"Yeah, I'm pretty sure that blood was a result of the abortion. I never got it checked out."

He nodded as I crossed my arms.

"Can I see the messages?"

"I've deleted and blocked most of them, all I have at the moment is the video of my car. I know the group that are sending them."

He looked angry as he put it all together in his head.

"That's what happened to your car?"

His voice was strong and deep, and sounded far more masculine that usual.

"I guess so." I looked down, ashamed. I handed him my phone and awkwardly looked at my shoes as I listened to the humiliating video playing as he watched.

He started pacing the room with his hands on his hips, sighing loudly.

"We have to do something. Have you contacted the police?"

"And tell them what? That I went up North for an abortion and now I'm getting stick for it? I'm pretty sure that's illegal, Ró."

"Yeah but this happened weeks ago. Aside from the harassment Ellie you were raped and you need to report it. Even if you could just report that much."

"I can't prove anything. He even denied it to me, as if I wasn't there. Like he was trying to convince me that it didn't happen."

He was getting angrier now, pacing faster and swearing under his breath. I regretted telling him so much of what happened at once.

"Look, I shouldn't have said anything. Please, can we just pretend I never told you? I just want to forget about it now."

After a few more paces of the floor, he breathed a heavy sigh, and sat down beside me. He put his hand on my freshly bleached platinum hair, pulling me into his scrawny chest, and kissed my forehead.

"Fine. This is your thing. When you're ready to talk, talk. I'll be here."

After a long pause he broke the silence with a stifled laugh.

"That was very *gay*, wasn't it?"

I laughed and nuzzled into him.

"Yes, very."

November 18th, 2014.

13.30pm

I paced the corridor outside the exam room and recited my lines to myself over and over. My hands were shaking and I could hear my voice quivering with nerves. Running one hand through my dark roots, I exhaled a lung-full of air in an effort to calm down.

Ró appeared behind me, and shook my shoulders.

94

"You'll be great. Relax. Think of the pints afterwards."
He was practically singing as he spoke.

"You've already finished your exam, of course you'd
say that."

"Yes and it went fine, even though I did no work at all.
You've been going over this for weeks now." He
snatched the sheet of paper from my hands and leaned
against that wall. "That's enough now, you're only putting yourself off."

Before I could protest, the door opened and the girl who
was being examined before me walked out, looking relieved.

He pushed me forwards, and wished me luck. With his
hands on my shoulders, he whispered that he would be
waiting for me in the beer garden of the pub across the
road.

One shaky monologue later, I went to meet him across
the road, and found him sitting in a cloud of smoke, created by a group of our fellow drama students.

"Well?" he called at me as I approached the group "how
did it go?" he handed me an ice cold pint and I took a
gulp before saying anything.

"Great" I sighed with relief and took another sip. "Two more written exams and I'm done"

We sat in a group of relieved drama students. When I had finished my pint, I offered Ró another round, and went towards the bar when he accepted.

I leaned against the wooden bar and tried to get the barmaid's attention. Her ponytail swung around and revealed Anna's smiling face. My heart stopped.

"Can I get you anything?" she acted as if she was pretending not to know me.

"Anna.." I prompted in a surprised tone. She pretended to only then catch on to the fact that she knew me.

"Oh my god Ellie! Sorry I did not recognise you with that hair- it's gorgeous. When did you do that?"

I shot her a look. "About a month ago, I don't know. How are you?"

"Yeah I'm great, I've just been so busy honestly. With work and college. Sorry I haven't been in touch much." She forced a weak, fake smile. I rolled my eyes.

"Yeah. I'll have two Heinekens please."

She gave another meek smile and turned around to get two pint glasses that had been through the dishwasher too many times.

"You know I haven't spoken to Jessica either" she said when she was back. "Honestly. I've fallen out of touch with everyone." I was cautious of the tone she was taking with me, going straight to explain why she hadn't been a friend to me lately.

"Yeah that sucks really." I was cold. I felt I needed to be. We had gone from a group of three best friends to three strangers, one of whom was vandalising my property. I was sure there was no coincidence that it had all happened in the space of a few weeks.

"How much will that be?" I asked as I took up one of the pints.

She looked around.

"Take them. It's fine."

I raised the second pint up to her in an effort to say thank you and that we were okay, and walked back out towards Ró.

He met me with an awkward guilty smile.

"You know how you told me not to do anything."

I stared with a blank expression as I sat down.

"Anything about what?"

"Well."

He turned my phone towards me, showing me my screen. It was a message from Jessica.

You are one psycho bitch.

"Ro, what did you do?"

He pulled out his own phone, and showed me a dark photo.

I could make out that it was of Ross's car- I recognised it from the night I asked him for the money. Right on the back, exactly the place where it was on mine, was some white marker with a string of profanities scribbled on.

"I'm sorry." He shrugged slowly

"No, you're not." I laughed

"You're right. No I am not."

I smiled up at him, appreciating his attempt to stand up for me.

"I'm sorry it spurred on more messages. I didn't really think they would be smart enough to think it came from you."

"It's fine. Technically *I* didn't do anything so. They can't say anything."

He took his pint from me and gulped it down.

December 6th, 2014

9.15am

My brother yelled down the phone at me.

"It's been weeks Ellie, you need to get me the money. I've been nice, I have. But you need to get it to me."

I felt awful. Between college work and the harassment that I had been receiving, I had completely forgotten about the money.

"I'll transfer it through this week, I promise. Please don't tell Dad."

"If you don't have it back to me this week, I'm going to have to. 1,000 euro is a lot of money."

As soon as the phone call was over, I checked my bank account and saw my balance of 300 euro. Without a second thought, I typed in my brother's details and transferred all of it to him immediately and sent him a text to let him know.

There was no doubt in my mind that if I had actually borrowed money for my car insurance, that my parents would happily pay for it. I didn't blame my brother for threatening to tell them either. However, they would be far less inclined to lend me 700 euro with no explanation at all.

Furious at myself for not looking for a job sooner, I knocked on my little sister's bedroom door. When there was no answer, I walked in and looked around. I went through her desk, her drawers and even checked under her bed. I didn't find anything.

Wanting to get the money situation out of the way, so that there were no more reminders hanging over me, I knew that I needed to move quickly.

The fact that Ró lived in a rented apartment with a studio doubling as a bedroom, and that he only worked two shifts a week in a real salon, I got the impression that he wouldn't be in a position to help. Judging by the abuse I was receiving from Ross's end, I gathered that he was never going to pay me what he had promised.

I decided that I wouldn't contact him, the whole reason I was rushing this process was so that I could pay off my brother and my parents wouldn't find out. No one else would know that already didn't, and I could put everything behind me.

December 6th, 2014
4pm

"Right so I have about 200 I can give you." Ró was trying to scrape together the money "So that means we would only have 400 left to make."
"Don't be ridiculous, I'm not taking any of your money."
He rolled his eyes, and looked down at our pathetic brainstorms in his notebook. We had crossed off borrowing, betting, stealing and selling jewellery.
"You'll take 100 from me. Alright, what about the guys from college? You could steal all of their drugs and then sell it back to them for a profit."
I laughed at the thought of stealing tiny overpriced bags of weed from our friends, but stopped when I noticed that Ró wasn't laughing with me. I raised an eyebrow in his direction.

"You aren't being serious, right?"

"I'm only half joking." His eyes lit up "why don't you ask them who they bought it from.." he was speaking slowly, as if he was only realising his plan with each word that he spoke. "..you could buy a large amount, and sell it off to drunk idiots on our next night out." He stared at me as if he had just solved a murder.

"Ró you can't be serious. Drugs."

His tone turned sassy. "I don't mean to be rude but what other option have you got at this point? What have you come up with that's better? And no offence but why haven't you got a job?"

I took a deep breath and considered the logistics of what he had just suggested in my head. He was right. I didn't have anything better.

"Fine." I said. "Fine, I'll buy it from someone and I'll sell it on for profit. Let's sit down and do the maths of how much we'll need to sell."

December 8th, 2014

10.30pm

After chatting with our obliging peers, we discovered that the dealer our college friends used was a 21 year-old from Howth. After a brief conversation via text, he agreed to meet me in a car park, where he would sell me a small bag of weed for €25. The plan was that then I would then get some information from him about where I could acquire a larger amount.

Ró sat nervously in the backseat as I drove along the coast road on the north side of Dublin. We drove in silence as he stared out the window at the palm trees that dotted the path, each one quickly disappearing behind us as we moved. He checked his phone for the map when we approached Howth.

"Ok it's just in here to the left."

I followed his directions and pulled up in an empty car park and switched off the engine.

"Right, hide. I'm going to call him"

He lay down on the floor in front of the back seat, and pulled a blanket over him. I made sure that my inside lights wouldn't switch on when the doors opened.

"Flash your lights, is that you in the blue Fiat?"

He sounded young and friendly over the phone, and I suddenly wasn't as scared anymore. I flashed my headlights into the darkness.

"There, I flashed them."

"Coming"

The line went dead.

"Jesus Christ Ellie you can't let him into the car!"

Ró was quivering in the back.

I shushed him.

The passenger door opened and a scrawny, wet hipster got into my car. He shook his long hair that was parted in the middle, and his tiny hoop earrings jangled as he did so. He wore blue corduroy trousers that were turned up so that they exposed his ankle, and black loafers- I couldn't see any socks. A gold chain dangled over a white T-shirt that was tucked in with a belt. His maroon bomber jacket was wet from the rain.

"I have what you wanted m'lady" he said as he handed me a small bag.

Taking the bag from him, I decided to go straight to the point.

"Listen, I was thinking of buying a larger amount than this, about 36 grams." I felt a kick in my back from Ró. "I was going to sell some of it to make back the money and then keep some for my own use" I lied.

He looked up at me and I noticed his beady brown eyes staring at me.

"That's insane. I haven't got that much, you asked for 1 gram in your text." He took the tiny plastic bag back from me.

"No of course I don't think you do, that's a lot to ask I know. Would you know where I could get that much?" I took the bag back off him.

"Why? Who sent you?" his eyes were panicked as he shuffled uncomfortably in his seat.

"No, nobody sent me. I honestly just want that much so I can make back some money and use the rest. Swear."

He looked at me for a few silent seconds, and then put his seatbelt on.

"Ok, Miss. Go out of the car park and turn right. "

Chapter 6

December 8th, 2014
10.50pm

The car jolted out of the car park, and I inched along the blackened roads. As he directed me, we drove higher and higher up the winding bumpy roads in silence. He asked me about college and about why I needed to make the money.

"I just thought it would be an easy way to make some money", I kept up my lie.

"There are easier ways to do that without distributing." He suggested. I felt another kick in my back from Ró.

"What way is that?" I asked, hoping his response would be something easier than selling of thirty-five grams of weed.

"Well the guy above me is always getting people to transport stuff that he isn't bothered to do. He's paranoid that the guards know what he's up to so he always makes other people do it for him. That's how I make most of my money, doing his dirty work for him."

I got the feeling from this guy that 'most of his money' wasn't a lot, but it was worth asking about.

"How much would you get and where would you have to transport it?"

He laughed. "It's not the Mafia. I get about 200 plus a gram or two for my own use just for cycling bags across town to where he stores it." Another kick in my back.

"I could move a large load for you. For 600."

He laughed at me, "No way, you're a girl. There's no chance I'm sending you off with my product. We just met."

I put my foot on the breaks. "I'm a girl?"

He started to panic "No, no I didn't mean that. I just meant that I don't know you, how could I trust you?"

"I'm a girl, so if I cycled or drove your 'product' across town, who on earth would suspect I was up to anything suspicious?"

I felt him grow less and less comfortable with the conversation as I went on.

"You're just pulling in here on the left" he signalled for me to keep driving up the road.

When I stopped the car outside a small house with a large gate, he took off his seatbelt and turned to me.

"So you'd drive a batch of weed across town and deliver it safely to the storage place for 600."

"yeah, of course. "

"And you don't want to distribute 35 grams anymore?"

I felt another kick in my back.

"No. I'll get more for transporting it for you. I can move a lot more with my car than you can on a bike."

"If you do this, you can't tell anyone. You need to drop it off and leave as soon as possible. They'll need to think it was me who delivered it."

Ró was now shuffling in the back seat. I turned up the radio.

"Of course, whatever you need. I'll do it for 600."

He bit his lip and ran his finger through his hair, thinking it over. Eventually he agreed.

"Ok. Fine. Send me your bank details. I'll run inside and get it. Wait here."

As soon as he closed the passenger door, Ró was up like a light.

"Are you fucking crazy? You're transporting drugs? This went too far Ellie what the fuck??"

"I'm not transporting drugs, I'm dropping a bag over to the other side of town and making the money I need doing it. Beats trying to sell 35 grams. Do I really look like someone who knows about drugs?"

"Ellie you need to drive away now I'm serious, you're not filling your car with drugs. Plus, he'll see me once you open the boot."

I hadn't thought of that.

"Get out then." He stared at me. "Get out, quick. Run down to the end of the road and I'll pick you up on my way back."

"Ellie it's lashing rain and freezing outside. I'm not getting out."

"Would you rather see his reaction when he realises I've been hiding a passenger the whole time?"

He sighed angrily in response and got out of the car.

I texted him as soon as I saw he had disappeared down the road.

I owe you.

December 8th, 2014

11.25pm

Finally, the dealer emerged from the gates, with a
rucksack, and signalled for me to get out of the car.
"Where's the rest of it?" I asked as he handed me the
bag.
"What do you mean?" he looked confused.
"How much is in here?" it felt heavy
"There's 100 grams." I stared blankly at him in response.
"Like nearly 4 ounces." He continued.
Having imagined I would be loading my Fiat with bags
and bags of drugs like I had seen on television, as my
brief encounter with drug transporting, I felt a huge wave
of relief.
"Oh. Ok."
He shook his head as if to laugh at me. "I've texted you
the address. Can you get it there tonight?"
I nodded as I flung the bag on to the backseat.
He fist-bumped me as a goodbye.

I found Ró sitting on a wall sulking at the end of the road. He didn't speak to me when he got in.

"I'm sorry. I just needed to get it done."

He rolled his eyes and looked around the car.

"Where is it?"

I laughed. He obviously shared the same naïve view of measurements.

Reaching back and lifting the small rucksack off the back seat, I threw it on his lap.

"That's it there."

He looked up in shock. "You're joking? This is it?" I nodded. "Why did I expect it to be far more substantial than this?" he burst into a fit of laughter.

"*This* is your big drug smuggle?" He stifled between laughs. "Oh, Ellie you crack me up."

December 8th, 2014

11.55pm

We followed the GPS to the drop off location feeling a lot less tense and lot more relieved. Our destination was an apartment in Dun Laoghaire on the opposite side of

111

Dublin. The route took us entirely along the coast so we had our windows rolled down to feel the cold sea breeze. When we stopped at a set of traffic lights Ró handed me a cigarette.

"Look at you" he teased as he lit the end for me. "Driving along the seafront with your bleached hair blowing, at midnight with a bag of narcotics on the backseat. Who *is* she?"

I rolled my eyes as I exhaled out the window.

"This is the only time we are ever doing something like this."

He nodded in response. "You can say that again. Here, give me your phone, I'll block that guy's number" he said as he reached for my phone on the cup holder to my left.

"No." I took the phone onto my lap. "Not until he has transferred me the money."

He clicked his tongue and shook his head.

"Look what we have done to the girl."

December 9th, 2014

00.25am

Half an hour later we arrived. I punched a sleeping Ró to wake him up.

"Wait here, I'm just going to ring the bell and leave it at the back door."

He yawned and blinked heavily at me. He squeezed my hand.

"Don't be crazy. I'll do it."

I drew a breath to protest but he was already out the door with the bag before I could move.

I watched as the shadow cast by my headlights grew longer and longer as he walked away from the beams and disappeared around the back of the white building. He dragged his clunky black boots behind him as he walked. I felt bad for what I had led him to. I wondered what on earth I had done to deserve a friend like him.

113

February 15th, 2015

5.30pm

When I emerged from my lecture after my last class, I
was met with Ró at the bottom of the stairs.

The thing about him was, no matter how awful he had
felt the night before, he'd always come in the next day
with his goofy walk, full of smiles and enthusiasm, and
more often than not, had a new conspiracy theory or a
new song to show me. It was easy to forget about my
past when he was dissecting songs, by analysing their
meaning or chords. He'd always have a coffee or a
cigarette for me after class, and he never spoke about the
messages, the revenge, the money or the drugs. Not
once, since the night I had dropped him home after the
drop off.

After class as we walked around town smoking, he
opened up to me more about his sister and his home life,
and I turned my attention towards being his shoulder to
cry on. After he had gone a little too deep into his
personal life, he changed his tone.

"We haven't been out in ages Ellie. Come out later?"

Despite the fact that I was wrecked after a long day at college, the idea sounded appealing.

"Oh yeah? What's on?"

He stopped and looked at me awkwardly shifting uncomfortably from foot to foot.

"Well, there's a pride night on. It's on after the gay rights rally in town." He avoided making eye contact as his cheeks flushed pink.

There was a referendum being held the following May, so everyone could vote on whether or not gay people should be allowed to get married, so these rallies had become a regular occurrence. I regretted the fact that I had yet to attend one, and realized that the vagueness around his sexuality was probably at the forefront of his mind. Ró had always avoided talking about the subject.

"Of course. That sounds fun."

"I'll be over at nine then", was his goodbye as we walked towards our different buses.

February 15th, 2015

9.15pm

On the walk towards town, we shared a bottle of wine as
he played a song he had produced on his laptop, and
explained how he changed the different levels and
harmonies and how he created certain sounds. It
comforted me to watch as his curly mop bounced up and
down with every step he took, and listened for his
distinctive laugh between every few words. His perfect
innocence couldn't be tainted. He picked out which
sounds were from real instruments and which were
created by him online, and the more he spoke, the more I
found myself zoning out and focusing on finishing the
bottle of wine.

The bouncer stamped my hand on the way into the club
and Ró took my hand and lead me to the bar. The scene
was incredible. It was a predominantly male crowd, who
were freely dancing with each other. There were no
sleazy straight boys taking advantage of girls, there were
no groups of bitchy girls huddled in corners- everyone
was just there to dance. Ró and I danced together for

116

hours, until a thick layer of sweat had developed on both of our bodies. The night grew shorter and shorter and my best friend grew drunker and drunker.

In the early hours of the morning, I watched as Ró's sweaty body danced around in front of me, spilling his drink on me and almost everyone else on the crowded dance floor. Unsure whether or not he was entirely coherent, I grabbed his hand and pulled him through the sea of multi-coloured flags and glitter. He stumbled behind me into the smoking area.

"Have you ever voted before?" he shouted in my ear in a slurred drunk voice.

"No, have you?" I had only been eighteen just over a year, and hadn't even considered registering.

"Pfft." He hiccupped. "Who knows anything about politics?"

I laughed and held his limp body up and tried to get his eyes to focus.

"Are you going to vote?" I asked as he wrapped his arms around my neck and his eyes closed.

"mmhmm." was his response.

Realising he had become far too drunk, I began to think through how I would get him home in this state. Dragging him back through the dance floor and out of the nightclub, I decided he would stay with me. He stumbled along beside me cheering, high fiving whoever would participate on the way out.

February 16th, 2015
11.15am

Unsurprisingly, I awoke to the sound of Ró vomiting into the bin in my bedroom, and the smell of stale cigarette smoke. Unfortunately, it wasn't strong enough to mask the smell of his puke. I opened the window.
"How are you doing?" I asked as I rubbed his back and he wretched into the bin.
"How does it look like?" he looked up at me with his face still full of glitter, and a smudged pride flag painted onto his neck, and eye liner falling down his cheeks.
I went down to the kitchen and fetched him a glass of water and a slice of toast. When I got back, he was fully

118

dressed, his face cleaned and sitting on the edge of my
bed.

"Ellie?"

I handed him the toast and water. "Yes?"

He took a sip and pulled a face.

"Remember that thing I did for you, and we never spoke
about it again?"

I wasn't sure where he was going with this, or what he
meant.

"Sure, yeah."

"I have my own thing I want you to do, and I want you
never to talk about this conversation again."

He was dead serious and I was starting to worry about
what he could have been talking about. I nodded. He
looked at me with sad, hungover eyes.

"Can you just vote yes in the referendum?"

I laughed at him. "What are you talking about? Of
course I'm going to vote yes."

"No. Can you vote yes for *me*."

Immediately I understood what he was trying to tell me.
I remembered the night on the roof where I had assumed
he was gay, and how he had never officially told me

119

whether he was or not. In truth, it didn't matter whether he told me or not. I couldn't help but smile at him for thinking it was in any way a secret.

"Of course. I know you would do the same for me."

He smiled as he rose up from my bed and put on his coat.

"And we'll never speak of this again?"

"Ró there's no reason to keep this quiet. It really doesn't make a difference to anyone what you are or how you act. Did you not see everyone last night?"

He shook his head and repeated himself. "And we'll never speak of this again?"

I hugged him. "Speak of what again?"

May 23rd, 2015

9.15am

Sitting on Ró's shoulders with a whistle between my lips, I looked down at the crowds of people population Dublin Castle. Everywhere I looked I could see pride flags and banners. Couples were kissing, there were balloons spelling out the word 'YES' and there was a stream of bubbles floating above our heads. Below me, Ró was chanting along with the crowd, dressed head to toe in bright multi-colours. For years to come I would mock him about this one day he didn't wear black. I climbed down.

"We did it!" he grabbed my face and shook it with excitement. I laughed back at him.

"Now we just need to find someone mad enough to want to marry you."

He shoved me as he laughed. We began to walk with the crowd.

A layer of sweat had formed over his body, which was blending in with the tears on his face, as he waved his flag and sung along, celebrating his new right to get married. His hand gripped mine tightly.

As the day drew on, we had joined a group of five gay men who were all out celebrating together. It was beautiful to see Ró light up around them, and be content to have truly found his crowd. He wasn't keeping his secret anymore.

Despite feeling overwhelmed by emotion by the atmosphere, and I was supporting someone I loved being able to proudly marry someone they loved, I felt as though this was his thing to celebrate, with his people. I pulled him to one side.

"I think I'm going to head home now."

He pulled an exaggerated sad face.

"Boo. Won't you come for drinks with us?"

I could sense from his tone that he was okay with me leaving and was happy with his new group. I hugged him tightly.

"I'm so proud of you. Will you text me when you get home tonight?"

He kissed the top of my head.

"Of course."

I watched as linked arms and walked away. I was happy to share my best friend for the day.

25th August, 2015

8pm

Sitting on a sand dune alone, I sat listening to my playlist. I thought of going into my second year of college and how so much had changed since that time the year before. I watched as Ró hit a shuttle cock back at his 'just a friend' Jack with an old badminton racket we had bought in a charity shop that morning.

I lay back and closed my eyes.

"Wakey, Wakey!" Jack shook his wet hands over me, so the water would splash onto my sleeping face. I sat up.

"Thank you- are you done yet?" I wiped my face with the towel.

They both laughed and sat down together opposite me. Ró draped his hands onto Jack's knee and rested his head on his shoulder.

Jack was a few years older than us, so was always fascinated by our college experience.

"So, are you guys excited to go back to school?"

"College, Jack. Are you guys excited to go back to college." Ró corrected him. "You're not that much older." They fell onto the sand in a bundle of tickles and laughter. I looked out onto the sea and was suddenly very aware of how single I was. Ró saw me looking uncomfortable with their public displays of affection. "Alright, alright. Let's not make her feel like a third wheel." They reluctantly peeled themselves off each other for my benefit. They attempted to engage in conversation with me.

"Are you on the apps?" Jack suggested, as if I was some desperate case.

"Apps?" I wasn't following.

"Dating apps. They are the most fun."

I pulled a fake smile and fiddled with my sunglasses.

"No, nothing like that happening here." I shotRó an uncomfortable look.

He understood and immediately changed subject to the options of what we could eat afterwards. I zoned out. It was then that I had my second flashback.

I was back in the apartment in Galway. I could feel his hands on me, guiding me to the couch. He was talking to someone but I wasn't sure if it was me, or what he was saying. I felt a pain in my back as he flung my limp body onto the leather and pulled at my clothes. My attempts to make any kind of noise were stifled by my inability to speak coherently. I heard a weak noise leave my mouth, only for him to press down on it with his palm to silence

me. My arms flailed about pathetically. I felt my eyes
closing as he fiddled with my shoes.

"I was thinking pizza. Ellie?"

I looked back at them and saw their confused

expressions look me up and down. I swallowed the lump

in my throat and asked them to repeat the question.

"We were just saying we might get pizza. Are you ok?"

Jack could see my obvious state of terror. I sensed that

Ró knew what was happening.

"She's fine, she's always zoning out like that. I think

pizza is a great idea. Will you run down to the takeaway

and order. We'll follow you down."

He looked at me with a half sympathetic, half worried

look. When Jack was out of sight, he turned to me.

"It's been a year. Are you ready to talk yet?"

I shook myself back into reality and began to clear up

my belongings.

"Yeah, pizza sounds great."

Chapter 7

September 3rd, 2015
6.30pm

Jack, Ró and I sat on my purple picnic blanket beside the canal, enjoying the last bit of sun we would get for the year. Ró sat with his bare legs crossed and was going on about his new favourite band, and the plans he had to give himself a tattoo of their new album's logo. Jack lay across his lap, with his legs extended out over the canal and looked up at him smiling like a lost puppy, appearing mesmerised by every word he said.

I had zoned out again and was watching the swans cutting the water on the canal into a smooth V formation as they silently glided along. They were uninterested in the bread and other small pieces of food that people were throwing to them from the banks. I sucked on my paper straw that had become soggy from feeding me my smoothie, and finished the rest of the sweet blend of raspberries and strawberries. I was brought back to the conversation when I heard them packing up their belongings.

"Where are you going?" I asked as I watched them empty the remainder of their coffees onto the grass. I shifted my sunglasses onto my head so I could clearly see them.

"*We*" Jack emphasised "are going to the pub because these coffees just aren't doing it for us anymore." He joked as he threw the empty paper cups into the large recycling bin behind us. "Come on."

Doing as I was told, I folded up my picnic blanket and shoved it in my handbag as I followed them towards town. They had a habit of ditching any plans we made halfway through for the pub, but as my skin was growing red from sitting in the sun a little too long, this time I was happy to oblige.

It was too early for bouncers to be working on the door so we walked straight in. Despite the early hour, it was loud and buzzing with people. It was my turn to find a seat, while the other two went to get drinks at the bar. I glanced around the crowded room and didn't immediately see anywhere available. I walked further into the

room and around the corner at the back to where a string
of booths with benches were. A tall lager drinker sitting
with two other boys caught my eye.

"Would you like my seat?" he offered as he stood up and
pulled out the chair. I looked at them. They were all well
dressed and smiled up at me, understanding my struggle
to find anywhere to sit.

"Thank you, but I have two friends coming too."

"Even better" he smiled and looked down to his friends.

"Male friends" I specified.

His two friends rolled their eyes in disappointment and
turned back to each other and resumed conversation.
After making a face at their rude reaction, he shook my
hand.

"Conor." He uttered with confidence. "Sorry about
them."

I lightly shook it back. "Ellie."

"Can I get you a-"

"My friends are already on it." I signalled towards the
bar to where Jack and Ró were trying to get the bar
man's attention. "But thank you."

After a glance over to see my friends, and noticing that

my companions weren't anything romantic he commanded his friends to move up the bench to make room for us.

My fingers tightened on the strap of my bag as I sat down beside him, my firm grip the result of not wanting to be awkward and take up room on the floor between our squashed legs. He pulled me up on it.

"What have you got in there?"

I loosened my grip on the bag as I looked up at him. His dark brown eyes were looking at my pink tote bag.

"Nothing important." I dropped it onto the floor "A picnic blanket."

The lines around his eyes creased as his face pulled into a smile.

"A picnic blanket." He repeated.

I nodded in agreement. "A picnic blanket."

"So you like picnics then"

"I do."

"And where would be your ideal picnic location?" he didn't drop eye contact as he spoke.

I cleared my throat. "A beach. The canal. A park. I don't know anywhere really. We were just out on the canal today."

His smile returned as he nodded and drank another sip of his pint.

"Good to know."

His friends had started their own private conversation, so the silence that had fallen wasn't quite as glaringly obvious.

"There you are!" I heard Jacks hysterical voice as he and Ró joined the table. Ró widened his eyes at me.

"So Ellie, introduce us to your new friends."

I opened my mouth to speak and turned to Conor. He had already extended his hand to shake Ró's.

"Conor." He said once again as he stood up and pulled a denim jacket over his toned arms and placed a cigarette onto the back of his ear. "We were actually just leaving. Ellie here was in the middle of giving me her number."

Ró's jaw dropped. "Well don't let us interrupt."

Conor looked at me and cocked his head one side with a hopeful grin.

I felt too awkward to discuss in front of my friends so I made the decision to move our conversation outside.

"If you'll excuse us."

Conor followed me out to the front of the pub and I turned to face him in the sun. With one hand in the pocket of my white sundress, and the other shielding my eyes from the sun, I looked him up and down. He was taller than me, but not quite as tall as Ró. His right hand was decorated with a shiny gold- coloured Casio watch, which stuck out underneath the denim jacket. He had that haircut that everybody had- short around the sides and long and wavy on top. He ran his fingers through it, seeing me looking at it.

"Why do you wear your watch on your right hand?" I asked, half teasing and half curious.

"Because I'm right handed" his response was quick.

"That's not how it works." I rolled my eyes.

"So Ellie who likes picnics, are you going to give me your number?"

I laughed at his label of me. "Fine. Give me your phone."

I took his smashed iPhone from him and keyed in my number, dodging the lines of broken glass. Echoing his cringy pet name, I saved my number as 'Ellie Who Likes Picnics".

His two friends emerged from the pub and waited at the doors for him. When he turned back from looking at them I handed him back his phone.

"Thanks. I can promise you a great picnic." He smiled. "Bye Ellie."

After he leaned over and left me with a polite kiss on my pink cheek, I walked back towards the doors of the pub and heard him shushing his friends jeering and mocking his approach.

Jack and Ró were practically pressing their faces against the window, squinting through the red patterned glass. Ró couldn't contain his excitement when I sat down beside them again.

"Tell us everything."

September 10th, 2015
6.55pm

"I hate it!" I threw the blue dress onto the bed and turned back to the wardrobe which then looked rather bare as half of its contents were strewn across my bed.

"Ok, go back to the shorts and black top" Ró instructed me.

Reluctantly I threw on the black Fleetwood Mac band T-shirt with my blue denim shorts. I turned to face him and he spun his finger, signalling for me to twirl.

"Your hair has grown out too much. Let me snip."

I grabbed my head in protest. "No way."

My bleached hair had grown out to just below my shoulders, enough so that it held one subtle wave. I let him keep my roots up to date every few weeks, but I refused to let him near it with a scissors again.

"Just let me at least blow dry it. "

I extended my finger at him and gestured to him to stay back.

"I mean it. I don't want him to think I tried too hard."

"I don't think there's any chance of that happening"

I rolled my eyes at him and clicked my tongue.

"Ok, I'm ready."

I slipped on my white runners, over my pink ankle socks, and swung my bag over my shoulder.

"Stop. Take off the runners Ellie."

He was standing behind me, with my beige sandals in one hand, and a white blazer strung across the other.

"He first saw you in a white sundress with make-up, maybe keep the runners for the third date."

My phone pinged and lit up a message from Conor.

I'm outside, x

I slipped off my shoes and pink socks, and strapped on my sandals.

"Ok. Now I'm ready."

A sharp spray splashed onto my face, causing me to cough with the taste of the bitter perfume. I spat.

"Oh God. I'm nervous."

Ró hurried me out the door and grabbed a bottle of Vodka he had left in my room the last time he was over.

"Take a shot of this."

Without thinking, I knocked a capful back and let the contents burn my throat. I grimaced at the affect. Ró beamed at me.

"Now you're ready"

September 3rd, 2015
7.05 pm

I opened the door and got into the passenger seat of his car.

"Did you bring your blanket?"

I held up my bag.

"Great."

The car jolted off out of my estate and down the road. I checked the rear view and saw Ró waving me off like a proud mother. Sliding a button back on the door, the sun-roof peeled back to allow the warm breeze to shake my hair. I looked over to him.

"Where are we going?"

"For the picnic you promised."

I laughed "Yes but where?"

He shook his head and pursed his lips. Looking into the back seat, I spotted a tote bag that had begun to bulge with its contents. I reached for it.

"Oi. No peeking." He grabbed my hand and placed it back on my lap, not taking his eyes off the road. He left his hand there.

"Oh come on, I can't know where were going or what's in there?"

"Nope."

I pulled my hair behind my head to reveal my thick gold hoop earrings and tied it in a loose ponytail. I sat back in the passenger seat and crossed my feet on his dashboard, glad that I Ró had made me wear the sandals.

After what seemed like just over an hour's drive, he eventually pulled the car into a winding road that lead to a dusty car park. Unwinding my legs, I took off my sunglasses and leaned forward to look out at our surroundings. I could see rusted silver railings around the car park, and layers of sandy dust. He opened his door. Reaching down to pick up my bag, he had already opened my door before I got the chance. I thanked him and got out.

He led me out of the car park through a secluded gateway that had been overgrown with plants and covered over with sand. I had to duck as we walked on the mossy path as branches and bushes hung into our walkway. Faded graffiti decorated the patches of broken wall that cropped up about every 15 meters. Eventually, after about 20 minutes of walking, we came to a small clearing.

"Have you got that blanket?"

I walked forward and took in the view.

The evening sun had disappeared and I was looking at a dull grey sky dotted with thin clouds hanging low and far away. The sea had begun to sparkle, as the moon had appeared to have taken over from the sun as the main source of light. I could both smell and hear the water. When I had finished staring at the beautiful view, I noticed he had walked further down the cliff onto a grassy patch and sat down, without the blanket. Slowly I walked down to him and laid out my purple blanket and sat on the edge.

"What have you got in the bag then?"

He pulled out two bottles of flavoured beer and a sketch-book. He tore out a thick square sheet and handed it to me.

"Draw me something."

I reached into the bag and pulled out some coloured pencils and poured the packet out onto the blanket.

"I can't draw."

"That'll make it more interesting then."

I looked around. I knew we had gone to the north side of Dublin, but I wasn't sure of where we were.

"Where are we?" I asked as I began to scribble some green lines on to my page, hoping I didn't sound ignorant.

"Do you really not know?" he looked puzzled that I didn't know his secret spot. I shook my head.

"We're in Howth."

I tried to hide my reaction, as I thought back to my only other experience with Howth which involved a small bag of drugs. It looked a lot more beautiful than last time.

I looked at his page, and watched as he drew long curved lines, joined them together and shaded them in with a palette of light mint-blue colours. I panicked and started to draw a few daisies on some green grass like I did in primary school, probably the last time I had drawn something.

"Are you in college?" he asked, not breaking his concentration as his blue pattern developed.

"I am. I'm studying drama. Are you?"

He looked up from his art. "Drama? You don't look like a drama student."

"Thank you?"

"It's a good thing. I graduated a few years ago. I studied business and economics."

I hadn't realised he was old enough to have already graduated. I wasn't sure how to ask his age without seeming rude. Obviously thinking the same thing, he beat me to it.

"What year are you in?"

"I've only just started my second year."

He smiled and didn't seem bothered by the age gap.

"Sweet. And are those guys you were with in your course too?"

"Just Ró is, the other guy with us was his boyfriend I guess."

He looked up at me "You guess?"

"They don't really like to use labels or anything, but he's as good as a boyfriend at this stage I think."

He let out a little giggle. "I see."

September 3rd, 2015

11 pm

The grey sky had now turned pitch black, and the grass had become damp. The beer bottles now lay empty around us and our bodies had gradually grown closer as the temperature dropped. In front of us lay our two pictures- mine a pathetic series of daisies in a row, and his, an intricate paisley pattern with all kinds of blues and greens as the theme.

Over the course of the night I had figured out he was working in an office in town at a job that I didn't fully understand but nodded politely and let on like I did. He walked from his apartment in to town every day, it was a short twenty-minute commute. We had little mutual friends or crossovers in interests in common but I felt comfortable and safe with him.

"We should probably get going soon, it's gotten dark without us realising."

I heard his voice break the silence and I turned to him. His face was suddenly right next to me. His brown eyes were looking at mine as a small smile cracked across his mouth, a quiet laugh escaping through it.

I could smell the minty chewing gum as his face came even closer to mine. I felt the cold tips of his fingers on the back of my neck as he pulled me in. His lips touched mine slowly, his mouth warm and inviting. He quickly pulled away and placed his other hand around my back and pulled me onto his lap. I wrapped both of my arms around his neck like a schoolgirl and leaned in to kiss him again. It felt empowering to be the one to kiss him this time, like I was in control of what was happening. He kept his hands firmly on my back and didn't dare move them anywhere, making it clear that if I wanted the situation to progress anywhere, I would have to be the one to do it.

I pulled away and held his face in my hands. A small smirk appeared on it as his hands began to tickle my sides, sending my wriggling off his lap.

"Come on, I'll drive you home."

"What about these?" I held up the empty bottles before placing them into my bag.

"Read it." He clapped back at me.

I turned one of the bottles around and read the label. *0% alcohol.*

"What? We've been drinking non- alcoholic beer?" I laughed at the thought of my one shot of vodka before I left being the only thing to calm my nerves.

"Of course. Don't want you getting me drunk and having your way with me on the first date." he joked as he folded up the blanket and signalled for me to lead the way.

If only he knew the significance of that joke.

Chapter 8

December 18th, 2015

11am

The cold breeze cut the top half of my face as I battled against the wind towards home. Thankfully, I had wrapped my oversized grey tartan scarf around myself before leaving to protect the bottom half of my face. I could feel my thick socks slipping down in my boots, my black tights creating an uncomfortable friction under them. Not wanting to remove my frozen hands from my pockets to fix it, I continued on, hoping to avoid blisters. My exams had finished the day before, and I had been off celebrating into the early hours with Ró. Having woken up with a headache on the floor of his little private hair studio an hour previously, the ice-cold air was not a welcome way to start my day. Noticing my hands beginning to tremble from a combination of freezing and of my lack of food or caffeine, I made a quick decision to stop in the nearest café for a solo morning coffee.

The warm air hit me in a breeze as I pushed my body against the thick door and shoved it open. Peeling my itchy scarf off me, I sat down on the first free bench, and ordered my coffee from a waitress who's friendly face was decorated with tasteful piercings.

My head was cloudy from the night before, so I lay back against the wall and closed my eyes. Without my vision, the sounds of the café became clearer. The clanking of my neighbour's teaspoon hitting the edges of her mug as she stirred her milky tea, the buzzing of the coffee machine as the barista made my order. Each individual conversation drowned out into one big merged echo, the radio was playing from a large speaker above my head. The sound of footsteps drawing closer caused me to open my eyes to see my coffee placed down in a neat white cup in front of me, a little free badge with it beside the brown sugar packet on the side.

Immediately picking up the badge, I turned it over, to see that it revealed a black circle with the letters YES printed on it. I looked up at the waitress.

" 'YES', thank you. Very cute." Seven months on from the referendum, there were still posters, badges, flags and other pride paraphernalia going around Dublin in celebration. They were usually brighter and happier, displaying the seven colours of the pride flag, I had never seen a black one like this before. I attempted to hide my hangover as she pulled out her card machine. "We did it." My comment was forced and awkward.

Instead of being met with a polite smile or a signal of solidarity, the waitress shot me a confused look.

"We did what?"

Unsure of how she could have misunderstood, I lifted the badge. "This. The right to marriage for everyone. 'Vote Yes'." I let a nervous laugh escape.

She shook her head. "Oh, sorry. This one is for the 8th Amendment. A lot less colourful than pride." My expression was blank. Her face turned from confused to impatient. "Campaigning for our government to call a referendum so we can vote to have the amendment changed?" She continued. I had no idea what she was taking about, but my ignorance coupled with a hang-over made the situation a little more awkward than it needed to be.

"Sorry, of course. I just haven't seen this kind of badge for it before, my bad."

Her polite smile returned as she handed me the machine to insert my card. "We have hoodies and tote bags over there too" she signalled towards the back wall, where an array of black merchandise with the word YES printed in white lettering across it was propped up for display. The machine beeped and my receipt began to print.

"'I'll have a look on my way out. Thank you." Placing the receipt with my card on the table in front of me, she shot me a patronising smile and went back to the counter. I fiddled with the badge in front of me and took a slow sip of my coffee. Immediately, I felt the taste buds on my tongue tickle as I swallowed the mouthful before it had cooled.

I wondered what the 8th amendment was, or why this girl felt like it should be repealed. Should I want it to be repealed? I had only voted once, and never really kept up with any other political issues other than that. In my defence, the previous referendum directly affected those around me, and was an almost unanimous no-brainer to vote Yes, but I made the decision not to take any more badges or cute little tote bags from the café before researching the campaign some more.

On my third gulp of my sugarless coffee, curiosity got the better of me and I found myself googling "Ireland's 8th Amendment." Sure enough, when I pressed enter, images of black backgrounds with the white YES or the word REPEAL filled my screen. I scrolled down to read about it.

The Eighth Amendment of the Constitution Act 1983 amended the Constitution of Ireland by inserting a subsection recognising the equal right to life of the pregnant woman and the unborn.

My eyes read the long words but my brain couldn't understand them. I read over them again, and this time the important ones stuck out.
…the equal right to life of the pregnant woman and the unborn.
The words *pregnant* and *unborn* sent my body into a defensive numbness. I scrolled down. The vibrations of my quaking thumb caused an accidental click into a linked article explaining further.

The eighth amendment is a clause inserted into
the Irish constitution after a referendum in 1983. It
recognises an equal right to life for both mother and
unborn child, effectively prohibiting abortion in all
cases.

A small lump gathered in my throat as the screen grew
blurry as a result of brewing tears. Clicking my phone
off I quickly lifted my cup to my trembling lip and drank
four consecutive gulps in an effort to mask my tears and
prevent a further reaction in public. Staring straight at
the out-of-focus wooden table in front of me, I then
lifted the badge and again read the word YES in thick
white font.

My first thought was of the momentum the previous referendum gained, and how many people rallied and pro-
tested for years until it had taken affect. How long was
this campaign going on? Who was behind it? Did people
really feel strongly enough to do something about it? I
had never even questioned the fact that I would have to
travel to the UK to have the procedure done, it was just a

given.

My mind was reeling with all of these questions I was silently posing to myself. Suddenly my mind wasn't the only thing that was reeling. A sharp pressing on my tummy and a small burp caused my immediate dart for the bathroom to my right.

December 18th, 2015
11.17am

My phone vibrated loudly on the bathroom floor beside me, the screen showing Conor's contact picture. It was a photo I had taken on our third date. I had met him for dinner in a Japanese restaurant in town, and he tried to impress me by actually using the chopsticks provided. I snapped him in an awkward scramble trying and failing to eat his sushi with them. The flash of my camera reflected on his watch. The call went to voicemail and my phone display changed to *1 missed call*.

I flushed the toilet, closed the lid and sat on it, staring at the green notification blankly.

Five minutes had passed, and I heard the door outside open, and a queue for the single toilet form. Unlocking my phone, I pressed dial and went back out to my table.

"Hello?"

"Hey" My voice was weak and shaky. I cleared my throat. "Would you mind picking me up?"

"Where are you? Are you ok?"

"Yeah, I'm fine. I'm just too cold to walk home and I have no change for the bus."

"Yeah sure I can just swing by and collect you on the way. I'm coming to your house for *brunch* anyway." His voice mimicked the word brunch that send him into an ironic cackling laugh. I ignored it.

"Thanks a million. I'll send you my location on Whatsapp now."

The line went dead and I send my location as I sat back down on the bench. The waitress walked cautiously to-wards me. I expected her to ask me to give up my seat for another customer.

"Is everything ok?" her tone was a lot warmer now, and I could sense that she knew I had just been sick. If she had come any closer she would have smelled it.

"I'm fine, thanks."

She glanced behind her before sitting down on the chair opposite me.

"Is it about the badge? Did I offend you?" her eyes stared at me through thick dark rings of eyeliner.

I realised the badge was still face up in the middle of the table, not on my jumper or bag or something cute like it was supposed to be.

"No, not at all. Honestly it's not that -"

"Because if that offends you, you should think about the women who have to resort to that. Twelve women per day. Twelve."

The lump in my throat returned, she wasn't correcting me, she was trying to educate me on something I already knew all about. I one of the twelve, nothing but a per-centage, a figure in her little agenda.

"That's not what I was saying, honestly I don't care about any of that. I'm sure this rule really offends those girls."

She wrinkled her face. "It's not something I want to shove down your throat, but I just think if anyone is sensitive to it, then they are missing the point. It's not something to ignore or dismiss because it is upsetting to think about, it's something we have to campaign to change. I bet someone you know has been in that position and you don't even know it. It's so much more common than you would think. "

I could hear her words and her genuine intention, but her ignorance was what started to annoyed me. I stared at her in silence, not wanting to react and cause a scene. She was still speaking.

"Really, all women should be allies."

Her condescending tone set off something inside me, so I leaned over to her and lowered my voice.

"Look, I don't mean to be rude, but I am one of those girls. And I am sorry if seeing something spelling out the word YES in block capitals, making something so awful into something to celebrate and campaign for upsets me. I don't want particularly want to be reminded of that time and I don't want some random waitress who doesn't know me, or know what she's talking about to patronise me. I'm just trying to have my coffee here. No offence."

She stared at me sympathetically and slowly shook her head. Standing up while she cleared my cup away, she slipped the badge towards me.

"I am sorry you had to go through that. When you change your mind, you know where to find us." She nodded her head in the direction of the merchandise stand.

I rolled my eyes and stood up to leave.

"If. Not when."

December 18th, 2015
11.36am

The left indicator lights flashed on my half-brother's car as he pulled in at the side of the road where I stood waiting. After the conversation with the waitress, I wanted a shower and to jump into bed, so I figured a lift from him would be the fastest way to get this.

"Well, where were you?" he pried as I climbed into his maroon Jeep.

"Just at a friend's last night. Nowhere interesting."

He turned on the radio. "A male friend's?" he suggested further, trying to get any incriminating material to bring up at brunch in front of the rest of our family.

"Yes, a male friend. You know Ró."

I could practically feel his eyes roll as he sighed in disappointment at the lack of any interesting social life.

"Fine." He gave up, turned the radio up and drove towards home.

December 18th, 2015

11.55am

Before my mother could get to me and ask me the usual string of questions about the night before, I ran two steps at a time straight up to my room and closed the door. After pulling the cheap silver hoop earrings out of my ears, I slipped off my boots and pulled down my tights to reveal two large blood blisters on the heel of my left foot. I dragged a dry cotton ball across them to remove the excess blood and then proceeded to remove my layers of clothing one by one. Standing in front of the mirror, I

154

reached behind me and unclipped my bra which revealed deep red lines on my pale skin from the tightness around my breasts as it fell on my feet below me. I kicked the black lacy torture device towards the laundry basket and flung my naked body onto my bed and closed my eyes. The feeling of relief after removing my slept in, restricting, uncomfortable attire was short-lived, as my mind was quickly invaded by the thoughts of my inescapable secret that apparently was going to continue to follow me even a full year later after it had happened. My chest grew heavy and my breathing slowed as I allowed all of my bottled up feelings to present themselves for what they were.

On the surface, there were the initial feelings of being violated, feelings that I had successfully suppressed, but had yet to fully disappear. Then came the aftermath of the hasty decision to terminate my pregnancy without fully considering what I was doing. I had then been subjected to bullying and the loss of my school friends, and had at one point even questioned my own sanity. After overcoming all of this, I felt defeated and hopeless that now I had this reminder of it all about to resurface. I

155

steered my thoughts towards what the girl in the café was addressing- the fact that I had to travel to take care of it. It had caused some internal complications that resulted in excess blessing on my first day of college, I remember that much. I hadn't been able to go to a doctor to check it out, for fear of being reported. It would have been a lot easier to pay a reasonable amount in my own country, rather than have to borrow so much and find dangerous ways to repay it. But was that my right? Did I have the right to do that? Like the girls in England? Thankfully, my spiralling thoughts were interrupted by my mother banging on my door to alert me to the fact that 'brunch' was starting. I hopped into the shower and I hoped that the new campaign would disappear, and that the hot water stinging the open blisters on my heels would be the only extra pain I would have to endure for the next while.

December 18ᵗʰ, 2015

12.30pm

After my brother had left, and my dad and sister had disappeared to their rooms, my mother stacked the dirty
plates and carried them over to the dishwasher, as I
cleared away the glasses and cutlery.

She chose this time to investigate my life.

"So, how did your last exam go?"

I placed the glasses beside the sink and walked back towards to table to remove the tablecloth.

"Great, actually. I'm much better at the practical exams
than the written ones."

I could see a smile crack on her lips as she emptied the
leftovers into the bin.

"That's great, well done. And how long have you got off
now before you go back?"

I knew that she was just trying to make light conversation and to be somewhat involved.

"We have a month off for Christmas so you'll probably
be sick of having me around so much."

I heard her warm laugh across the kitchen. It lingered in

the air as the conversation fell silent and we both continued to clean up after the meal. After a few moments, I
could hear her pause and turn to me.

"I saw the maddest thing yesterday on the side of a bus."

"Oh yeah?"

"Yeah. A picture of a foetus with the words Pro Life on
it. A foetus." she practically shuddered at the word.

I didn't say anything, so she continued on to fill the silence.

"How did they even get a picture of a foetus?"

The thought of that did make me laugh a little.

"It was probably just computer generated, mom. I doubt
it was a real foetus."

"Whatever, I still thought it was really graphic and inap-
propriate to put on the side of a bus. Children can see it
there."

I decided to play dumb, but after my morning encounter
in the café I had a good idea of what she was talking
about. "What does pro-life mean?"

"I'm guessing they are protesting against the campaign
to get abortions." She was so blasé about the word.

Abortion. That gave me hope that this might be the time to tell her about what happened.

 "Which is fair enough, but don't put such graphic pictures on the side of a bus."

My heart sank. It wasn't fair enough.

"That's very strange. What do you think of it all?"

She stopped what she was doing, put her hands on her hips and thought for a moment before answering.

"I think it's pretty selfish. Imagine, if I had an abortion we would never have had you or your sister. Look at your dad. Before he met me, he got his girlfriend pregnant very young, imagine a life without your older brother."

I wasn't sure how I felt about what she was saying. I agreed that I couldn't imagine a life without my siblings, but it wasn't a fair analogy because she didn't need to have an abortion.

"What about in the cases of people who are raped? Say like, I don't know, a 15 year old girl gets pregnant from a rape or something."

She raised her eyebrows and heaved a heavy sigh.

"That's an awful situation. But I don't think it happens often enough to justify suddenly having abortions here. The extreme cases can go to England for that. People would be using it as contraception. Honestly."

Her eyes rolled as she wiped down the counter and pottered around the kitchen. I stood expressionless facing her while I mulled over the conversation we had just had.

The extreme cases. That was me. An extreme case. A case, a figure, a statistic. I wonder if she would have thought differently if she knew that her own daughter was a part of that. At least for the moment though, I was too afraid to find out.

Chapter 9

February 14th, 2016

9.15pm

The red wine had caused my teeth to turn a dark shade of
purple, and a residue of black gunk lay in a creased line
across my bottom lip. I dabbed at them with a folded
piece of tissue and reapplied my lip liner, finishing it
with a thin layer of gloss. Deciding the rest of my make-
up was presentable for the moment, I tucked my short
white hair behind my ears so my earrings were on show
and rubbed the tiny free sample of perfume I had brought
with me on my wrists and neck. Not being used to wearing heels, I stumbled a little as I checked myself in the
full length mirror before leaving.

Walking back out to the bar, I could sense I was a little
drunk, which made me extra conscious of the possibility
that I may fall over in my heels. As I approached our table, Conor lifted his head from his phone and greeted me
with a smile.

"You're back." He clicked his phone off.

Putting my handbag on the table in front of us, I took a
sip from my wine glass.

"I'm back." My fresh lip gloss left a stamp on the rim of
the glass.

"We are about three drinks deep and you still haven't
guessed what day it is today."

I picked up the single rose wrapped in a sheet of plastic
with pink crepe paper he had picked up for me earlier on
Grafton Street. It was a giveaway.

"What are you talking about? It's Valentine's day."

I tilted the flower towards him and touched it off his
nose. He lifted the flower off me and placed it on the table with my bag.

"Yes. But what else is today?"

I panicked, and began to scan my memory for any significant dates he had mentioned. His birthday was definitely in July. When I didn't immediately answer, he
sensed my confusion and panic. He cleared his throat before prompting me.

"We've been dating for six months today."

I let out a sigh of relief, glad that I had not forgotten an
actual milestone.

"Oh God, Conor you scared me, I thought I had forgotten something actually important."

His smile turned sour as he mimicked an angered expression. "What are you talking about? I was going to propose." He lasted another two seconds before he broke character and let his laughter spoil the sarcastic act.

I leaned in and kissed him, my freshly applied lipstick leaving a burgundy smear across his lips.

"Sorry, I'll fix that."

I dragged my thumb across his bottom lip and leaned in to kiss him again. I could feel his chuckle as his mouth quivered under mine. He muttered something between kisses that I couldn't hear. I pulled away.

"There not much point in rubbing it of if you're just going to kiss me again." he eventually managed to say without interruption.

"Fine, I'll stop." I pulled away and took another sip of my drink. "Do you want to go somewhere else?"

"What's wrong with where we are?"

"Nothing, but maybe we'd want a change of scenery."

There was a short pause before he casually brought up the subject.

"Do you want to come back to mine?"

His question lingered in the air like a pink elephant in the room. As he had previously pointed out, we had been dating for six months, and I was suddenly very aware of the fact that we hadn't slept together yet. Initially, this had started out as a coincidence- the opportunity had never presented itself. After a few weeks, he began to gain confidence and move his hands lower and lower when we kissed, and he had offered me a place to stay with him on multiple occasions. I realised his intentions but in reality, I hadn't even thought about going there with anyone since... what happened. It wasn't that I was completely opposed to the idea of sleeping with him, but more that I hadn't decided on where I stood with it. I kept reminding myself that the last person who had sex with me was a rapist. That was just it though; they had sex with me. I didn't have sex with them. To be honest, a part of me wanted the slate wiped clean, but another part of me was terrified something like that would happen again. I trusted Conor, but it wasn't about whether I trusted him enough. In truth, I didn't trust myself or how I would react. The last thing I wanted was to break down in front of him or make a huge issue of something that wasn't a big deal to anyone else our age.

Realising the silence, I pulled myself away from my thoughts and looked at my date sitting nervously looking at me. He was the only boy I had ever heard of to wait six months before making a move, without complaint. I figured he must be genuine. In response to my trailing off into an awkward silence, he tried to take his offer back.

"Or if you just want me to walk you home that's ok too I guess."

The way he spoke portrayed him as a sad puppy, but not in a manipulative way. Making the decision to trust him, I made a mental note of not finishing my glass of wine before leaving, so at least I had some sense of control of the situation.

"No, I'm too tired to walk. Let's stay at yours."

A smile reappeared across his face and I swear I saw him choke a little on his pint.

"Great." We left our drinks three quarters full and left immediately.

In the taxi, he sat holding my hand in the back, making light conversation with the driver. His thumb anxiously rubbed the back of my hand and his knee rapidly bounced up and down as he spoke. The two voices muffled together into one merged noise as I stared out the window and breathed slowly in an effort to slow my heartbeat down. Conscious of my hand beginning to sweat, I pulled my hand away and pretended to text someone on my phone. Knowing that he would probably see that I was faking, I took the opportunity to check in with Ró. I pulled up Whatsapp and began to type.

-*I'm in a taxi on the way to his house*

The message had barely delivered when he replied.

-*Oh my god, are you staying over?*

-*I think so, yeah*

-*Are you going to do anything?*

-*I have no idea, he doesn't know about anything.*

"You can just let is out anywhere here, thanks so much." Conor's voice brought me back to reality. I looked up, and saw him hand the driver ten euro and open his door to get out. I put my phone back in my bag and took a deep breath. As soon as he had walked around to my side of the car, he held my hand immediately and led me along the grey path in a cute little neighbourhood with long terraced houses. The clicking of my heels was the only thing that broke our silence.

"I'm just in here."

He stood back and gestured for me to walk ahead of him towards his front door. My knees were shaking at the thought of him watching my awkward walk in heels towards his house. The gate squeaked as he pushed it open and I approached his door. I could feel his hand on the bottom of my back as we walked. The door clicked open as he turned the key in the old lock, and he lead me by the hand into his front hall. I couldn't make anything out as it was dark, and my thoughts were elsewhere. I felt his arms wrap around me as I heard him kick the door shut and he began to kiss the back of my neck. Stumbling forward, I gigged as he pulled away and turned on the lights. We had made our way into the next room and the lights revealed a clean, bare kitchen with a dark brown leather couch by the window.

"Do you want to sit down? I can get you a drink?"

I looked around and my fear of being caught by someone through the curtain-less windows decided my answer.

"No, I'm actually pretty tired."

He took the hint and lead me back out of the room towards the stairs.

His bedroom door swung open and this time he didn't bother to turn on any lights. The dim light from the streetlight outside his window shone into the room revealing an unmade double bed directly under it. I sat down and watched him, my bag placed awkwardly on my lap. I didn't know what to do with my hands. The silence remained uninterrupted, apart from the bang of my clunky shoes hitting the wooden floor as he pulled them off me. Once he had done this, I swung my legs up onto the bed and lay down. He leaned in over me, and began to gently kiss me, his hands fumbling around me in the dark.

I refused to open my eyes. The moment was too fragile to risk getting triggered by previous experiences. I let him kiss me and remove my carefully planned outfit- my insecurities about my body seemed to disappear once we

were in the dark and I'd had a few drinks. I soon realised
we were both undressed and I began to panic slightly. I
opened my eyes and stared at his ceiling, and attempted
to reassure myself with affirmative thoughts.

He was different.

 He was not the same boy.

It had been over a year. I was safe. He waited six
months. I was sober.

He must have noticed my thoughts were elsewhere as he
pulled away and stopped.

"Are you ok?"

I felt around for his face and spoke to it.

"I'm fine. I just need to use the bathroom."

Before he could respond, I slipped out from under him,
pulled on his shirt from the floor and went straight for
his bathroom.

My reflection showed my make- up was smudged
around my face- my lip gloss had now completely disappeared. The back of my hair had begun to matte from
rolling around on his pillow. I had lost an earring. The
affirmative thoughts weren't working, I needed to think
of something else to calm myself down. In an effort to

prevent any negative reminders of my past from resurfacing, I emptied my brain and stared at my own eyes and breathed slowly and carefully. It was proving difficult to think of nothing.

February 14th, 2016
10.30pm

 I must have stared at myself for a long time attempting to think empty thoughts, because a knock at the door signalled that Conor was looking for me.
"Ellie? Are you ok?"
I refocused my eyes and caught the tears that were rolling down my face before running my fingers through my hair.
"I'm fine, just one minute."
As I opened the door, the bathroom light spilled out and illuminated his bedroom. He was clothed now, and looked at me as if to prompt an explanation for my disappearance.
"Have you been crying? Did I do something?"

I stepped forward and wrapped my hands around his neck before kissing his cheek.

"No, you didn't do anything. I've just got my period." He breathed a sigh of relief as he tightened the hug.

"Ah why didn't you say?" he clicked off the bathroom light, scooped me up like a baby and walked me back towards his bed.

"Do you need me to get you anything? Some tissues or…." His voice trailed off and I sensed that thankfully, he didn't know a lot about the subject. He gently dropped me down onto the bed and lay down beside me.

"No, I'm all sorted. I'm really sorry, I know you wanted it to happen tonight." I lied. It was the first time either of us had acknowledged the fact that we hadn't slept together yet out loud.

I felt him kiss the top of my head and roll me over towards the window to spoon me. I closed my eyes and felt a wave of guilt pass over me for lying to him, and not being brave enough to go through with it. There was a feeling I couldn't shake that I was letting him down and punishing him for someone else's crime. If i was honest with myself, his reaction and patience made me feel even

171

worse about the subject. Despite this, I couldn't help but feel a little sense of pride in myself for managing to prevent any flashbacks or trauma from taking over. Some minutes passed, and his breathing slowed and eventually moved to a gentle snore. Once he was asleep, I allowed myself to do the same.

February 15th, 2016
8.45am

I felt him pull me back in towards him in his sleep as I awoke. The window above me now gave way to the morning sun which shone onto my squinting face. I sat up. He stirred beneath me as I pealed myself out of the bed and walked out of his room.
The wooden floors were cold beneath my bare feet as I crept downstairs.
The clean kitchen from the night before now contained a dirty coffee mug, a used plate and a crumpled up tissue on the counter. Someone had also left a carton of milk out. I made it my job to clean this small mess as a way of making up for my sexless sleepover. As I cleared away

172

the mess, I was interrupted by a furry, purring creature weaving its way between my legs. I picked up the orange cat and put the kettle on.

When it had boiled, I made two cups of coffee in two chipped mugs. With the cat in one hand and two cups balancing in the other, I made my way back upstairs to my host.

When I arrived he had woken up and was sitting looking out the window. Once he heard the cat meow, he turned to face me.

"Ah. I thought you'd snuck out on me."

I let the small cat go and placed his mug on the bedside table for him.

"Never."

I sipped my drink and waited for him to address my sudden 'period' the night before. He didn't.

"I was thinking today we could go for a walk together, it's so nice out."

I looked over at my pile of clothes on the floor. They were not suitable for daytime walks. He saw me looking.

"I can give you some clothes, you can wear my shorts and a hoodie or something."

I admired his enthusiasm and felt after my mishap the night before, I should humour him and go. Placing my mug down on the table, I opened his wardrobe and scanned its contents.

"Alright, what have you got ?"

February 15th, 2016

9.30am

His grip was casual and loose on my hand and it swung slightly as we walked alongside the pond in the park opposite his house. His baggy grey shorts hung down to my knees and I had tucked a thick white t-shirt into it. I wore his white puffy jacket to keep warm, and his old over-sized runners flopped along like a duck as I walked. Before we left, he had raided his kitchen cabinet for some stale bread to feed the actual ducks, this hardened sliced pan swung in his other hand. We stopped when we reached a flock of ducks and began to break down the bread into small crumbs. I tossed a handful at them.

"How are you feeling this morning?" he asked as he threw the bread out onto the pond.

"What do you mean?"

"Your em…" he waved his hand at my general tummy area.

"Oh. That. I'm fine. Thanks." He didn't say anything.

"Sorry about that again." I continued.

He watched the ducks snap up the bread he had tossed.

"Don't be sorry. I'm just making sure you're ok."

I sensed that he knew I wasn't telling the truth but was too polite to press the matter. That was all that we spoke of it. After a while we began to shiver as the temperature had dropped since our arrival. Once we had finished distributing the bread to the eager crowd, he took me by the hand again.

"We'd better get back. I'm freezing."

Chapter 10

June 26ᵗʰ, 2016

6.30pm

A sea of dancing colourful bodies were filling Rós little
studio after the Pride parade. Even though I was sober, I
couldn't even make my way through the room when I arrived alone. It was chaos. There were banners being
sprayed, paint all over the floor, glitter all over bodies.
Hysterical grins pinned across each individual's face.
The studio windows were opened and the warm June
breeze wafted in onto us all. Despite its best efforts, it
didn't cool down the sweaty dancing bodies. A large
bowl full of punch with floating fruit and ice was
perched on a table in the corner of the room. I could
make out that Jack was handing out streamers, ribbons,
paint, hats and any other Pride merchandise that one
could make any kind of costume or flag with. Someone
to my left had just knocked over a large bucket of purple
glitter. The music was so loud the pounding bass sent the
particles of glitter flying into the air with each beat. I

waded my way through the pandemonium over to where Ró was sitting. In typical Ró fashion, he was wearing a tall multicoloured top hat with feathers sticking out of it- he resembled Jack Sparrow crossed with The Mad Hatter. As I got closer to him, I noticed he had a plastic champagne flute and beads around his neck.

"Elle! There you are. Come here." He waved his arms at me as I waded past the crowd. Moments later an accidental shove from a party goer forced me onto his lap. I wrapped my arms around him and as I did so he gave me a kiss on the cheek leaving a big lipstick stain on the side of my face.

"Do you want a drink? You don't look drunk."

I looked over at the communal punch and decided it didn't look very appealing.

"I think I'll pass on the punch, thank you."

He pulled out a bottle of wine from under his chair and opened the cap.

"Like old times." I took the bottle from him and unscrewed the cap. After two sips I passed it back to him.

"I am so gay that my own birthday coincides with Pride every year." He uttered between gulps. "I was never going to turn out any other way was I?"

I looked around the room, the whole scene was very reflective of his personality.

"Speaking of your birthday… Do you want your present?"

He pushed me off him in a shocked surprise. "You're joking. You didn't have to get me a present."

"Don't be dumb." I stepped up and lead him by the hand through back through the room. As he walked obediently behind me, he pulled on the back of my multicoloured striped bodysuit that I had paired with denim shorts. "I love this. How very Ally of you"

I had done my best to dress up for pride.

"Thank you" I replied as I wrapped a silky purple scarf over his eyes and tied it at the back of his head to block his vision. I held up two fingers in front of his face.

"How many fingers am I holding up?"

He cracked a smile.

"Hopefully not just the middle one."

We walked back out through the front glass door. Every time I walked through his front garden, I was reminded of the day I discovered that my car had been vandalised. Telling myself this was not the day for negativity, I put that out of my mind.

"OK, you can look now."

He frantically pulled the scarf off his face and stared at the present in front of him.

"No!" he squealed in delight and ran straight towards the turquoise bike with a golden wicker basket planted at the front. I had got it at a charity shop in town. "You've even got the flowers and everything!"

I felt happy tears fill my eyes, I was so delighted that he loved it. I felt I owed him something for all of the trouble I had put him through.

"Do you remember?"

He hopped onto the bike.

"Of course I remember. Quick, take my picture."

I whipped out my phone and took a picture of him posing on his new bike, just like the ones he had taken of me the night we first met.

"Oh God, Ellie this is so perfect. Sentimental and practical. I love it. Really."

He was cycling in circles around me.

"Hop on the front" he was far too drunk to re-enact that
part of the evening so I laughed at his suggestion.

"No, that didn't turn out too well last time. Besides I've
gained about seven pounds since then."

"Don't be ridiculous you're still a tiny little nymph."

Before he could convince me to jump on, Jack walked
out of the party with two plastic cups with the pride flag
on them.

"Here you go guys, some punch. Sorry Ellie, it's manda-
tory."

He stopped in his tracks when he saw Ró.

"Oh wow, that's a gorgeous shade of teal- Ellie did you
get this?"

I was secretly delighted my gift was a hit.

"I did, don't worry I'm sure I didn't out do your present
for the King on his birthday."

Jack rolled his eyes. "You just may have, that bike is
beautiful. Here, let me put the flowers in some water."

180

Ró blew him an air kiss as he took the cups off Jack and handed one to me. When Jack had left with the flowers he turned to me and lowered his tone.

"Ok, so when is Conor coming? How is everything going with you two?"

He dismounted the bike and locked it against the lamppost in his front garden with the I had placed for him in the basket.

"Not great to be honest. Well, yes great. He's amazing but we haven't exactly, you know.."

"No, sweetie I don't know, be frank. I'm drunk"

"We haven't had sex yet."

Ró raised one finger to me to signal for me to wait a second, took a sip of his drink and then proceeded to theatrically spit it back out in shock.

"You what?!"

A laughed escaped my mouth.

"Was that really necessary?"

"We're drama students, Ellie, play along for God's sake."

I rolled my eyes.

"Anyway, we've come close a few times but each time I chicken out." He nodded slowly taking it all in.

"Ok, I get you" I was glad that his tone was now serious "and do you think that that has anything to do with the whole Ross thing?"

I shuddered at his name. In his drunken state Ró had forgotten that I hated to hear it.

"Yeah. Well, kind of."

He shook his head at me as if to say he didn't understand what was happening.

"Well, I haven't had any flashbacks in ages. Months." I thought about it. "Actually, probably years. To be honest, I haven't felt scared or had any triggering feelings exactly. It's more the fear that it might happen again. Do you understand what I mean?"

He looked at me carefully as if he was playing it all out in his mind. "So, you haven't had any kind of trauma coming back from what happened before, but you're afraid that you might react that way if you go any further?"

"Kind of, yeah."

He shrugged and mulled it over in his head. "I know

that's really tough for you, and I'm sure it's causing a lot
of stress, but it's definitely better than experiencing
those feelings all over again around someone you love.
Do you not think you would have felt them by now?"
He had a good point, if those feelings hadn't presented
themselves by now, maybe they wouldn't. I continued.
"Once things develop,"
"*develop*" he interrupted me to make fun of my choice of
words.
"Once things *progress* to that point." I corrected myself.
"I spend the time focusing on actively trying to avoid
slipping back into that moment."
His tongue licked the inside of his lips as he thought it
through.
"That's counterproductive in my eyes. I know everyone
deals with things differently but I'm drunk so I'm just
going to tell you what I'm thinking."
"Ok, go on"
"It's been a year nearly since you've been together.
You're comfortable with him and you aren't getting
those feelings when you're in bed together or kissing or
whatever it is that straight people do."

I smiled.

"But" he continued " if you keep trying to avoid a negative experience, you're just giving Ross all the power. Ross isn't there in the bedroom with you. I think you should wait until you are ready and stop driving yourself mad. You can't force yourself to do something you're not comfortable with by actively banishing negative thoughts. Wait until you're ready."

It was astonishing that even drunk, Ró was always far more intelligent than me.

"I think that I am ready though. Really."

He cracked a smile. "Then take control. Change the situation. You lead the way." He nudged into me as he said that. "I think you've got it in you."

I nodded. "And please," he continued "-drink up. It's my birthday. You have to do everything I say."

I leaned back and swallowed the contents of the cup in one gulp. It tasted like soapy detergent.

"Ok, tonight's the night."

June 26th, 2016

9.45pm

The room around me spun as I danced around Ro's little studio with Conor. I admired the fact that he was always surprisingly comfortable in a room filled with both boys and girls belonging to the LGBTQ+ family. There were probably four other straight people here, all of whom were girls. Thanks to a lot of punch, I gained confidence and had started to grab his arms and put them on my body as we danced. We got a lot of sarcastic jeers at our outright straight behaviour on Pride. I drowned them out. After a few minutes Conor pulled away.

"I'm going to get another drink."

I watched him disappear as I continued dancing and checked the time. I was ready to leave. Ró had hyped me up and I was determined to make it happen that night. When Conor returned with more punch, I drank my drink down in record time.

"Jesus Ellie, slow down."

He took the cup from me. "I think you're drunk, Elle"

I wrapped my arms around him "I think you're right"

He spun me around and laughed.

"Let's go home." I said when I landed and the room stopped spinning. He looked confused.

"And leave Ró's birthday? He's your best friend."

We both looked over and saw Ró being hoisted up onto Jack's shoulders as he waved his champagne flute in the air to the music, drink spilling on anyone who passed.

"I think he's ok, Conor."

He shrugged back at me.

"Alright, if you say so"

"I do"

After saying our goodbyes, we left the party and walked down the estate together. I was stumbling, but in my head I was doing my best impression of a sober person.

"Come on, let's go get a taxi back to your house."

He took another look at me, obviously not convinced of my sobriety.

"If we do, do you promise me you'll have some coffee and toast?"

I nodded before breaking into a smile and mocking him.

"If we do, do you promise me you'll have some coffee and toast"

He must have realised my arms had begun to sprout tiny goose bumps as my body suit didn't cover very much skin. He pulled his arms out of his blue hoodie and draped it around me, before bundling me into the nearest taxi.

He climbed in beside me and gave the taxi driver his address.

I don't remember the taxi ride, but when we got there, I marched up to the door, stopping to kiss him along the driveway. We burst through the doors and to my disappointment he lead me straight into the kitchen, where he flicked on the lights and boiled the kettle. As he pulled down the coffee jar, I realised that he had no intention of sleeping with me while I was drunk.

Obligingly, I took his the slice of toast he offered and gulped down the coffee. He laughed at my eager attempt. "What's gotten in to you?" he asked shaking his head as he sipped a glass of water and leaned back against the counter.

"Nothing, I think that I'm just a little bit drunk."

"I can see that." He swirled his water and looked into the

glass. "What has you all over me tonight then?"

I knew he could tell my agenda.

"Nothing, I just hoped that tonight we could finally do it." I was blunt.

"Do you mind me asking why it hasn't happened yet?"

I suddenly felt very awkward and sobered by his direct question. He continued on "I don't mind if you just wanted to wait a bit, I'd just rather know."

I stared at him. He had completely killed the mood. I spoke slowly.

"We just never really had the chance." He didn't buy it.

"Bullshit. We've been together months. You clearly wanted to wait, which I have respected, and now suddenly you're all over me? I'm a little confused. Why tonight?"

Remembering Ró's pep talk, I made the decision to leave the past behind me right then and there. I wouldn't let Ross weave his way into my relationship and I wasn't going to let it hold me back any longer.

"I just had a very bad experience the last time. I was incoherent and couldn't consent properly and I was waiting until I felt like I could be completely in control of my feelings until I did it again." I stared blankly at him, shocked at the clarity and bluntness of my statement. He didn't respond.

"Conor?"

He didn't look up from his glass. His expression was mournful. A few moments passed before he responded. "Ellie, you should have told me that. I wouldn't have even touched you without asking. I feel awful."

I rolled my eyes and let out a huge sigh.

"No, this is the opposite of what I wanted to happen. It isn't your fault, I feel safe around you. It doesn't define me, and it shouldn't have decided when or who I was ready to sleep with."

He looked up at me.

"When did this happen?"

I walked towards him and placed his hands on his chest and leaned my face in towards his. "A long time ago." Hesitantly, he ran his fingers through my hair. "Does this make you feel ok?" I nodded.

"Does anything I do remind you of what happened?"

I leaned in and kissed him before he could continue. He pulled away and looked into my eyes, as if demanding an answer.

"Honestly Conor, I'm finding it hard to think of anything else but you right now."

He pulled away even further.

"Are you sure? Have you thought about this properly?"

I didn't respond, but lead him over to the brown leather couch by the window. As he timidly sat down, I carefully mounted his lap and leaned in to kiss him.

"Ellie" he interrupted "If you want to do this I'm going to need to hear you say yes. I want to be sure that you are certain about this."

I scanned his face. He looked back at me with his sympathetic, caring brown eyes. I didn't want him to do this because he felt sorry for me. However, the bulge I had caused in his trousers reassured me that he was game too. I stroked his bottom lip with my thumb in response.

"Yes."

June 26th, 2016

10.30pm

Ró's advice of taking the reins and adopting the role of the dominant one worked very well for me. For the most part of the whole ordeal I lead the way, established my boundaries and let him take a backseat, which he appeared more than happy to do. As we lay on opposite ends of the couch, our naked bodies glistening with a layer of sweat, I mulled over what had just happened. My overwhelming feeling of pride was a result of being relieved to discover that for me, in the end, it really was no big deal. Two years, a solid relationship and phenomenal support from my best friend was enough for me to overcome my fear.

My thoughts were cut short by my striped bodysuit being flung in my direction.

"Come on, we'll go up to bed will we?"

Wearing only socks, he stood up and stretched out in front of me. I jumped onto his bare back and he wrapped his arms around my ankles as they dangled around his sides.

"You want a piggy back ride up to bed?" his head shook in front of me as he laughed before obligingly walked me out of the kitchen and up the stairs to bed. Our clothes lay in piles on the kitchen floor, with some still strewn over the couch.

We made it to the bed where he dropped me down onto my back when I heard my phone ringing all the way back downstairs. Before I could tell him to ignore it, he took off like a light down the stairs, still naked.

A few moments later, he appeared frantic at the bedroom door, scrambling to throw on whatever clothes lay on his floor. He threw a hoodie at me.

"What's wrong?"

He was slipping runners onto his feet.

"Get dressed. It was Jack. There's been an accident. I'll order a taxi."

My whole body began to shake as my heart sunk right down into the pit of my stomach. Unable to speak or ask questions, I did as I was told and shakily put on the hoodie and a pair of Conor's GAA shorts. In silence, we hurried downstairs and out into the taxi, where we sat in the back seat holding hands. Just as before, my fingers

192

were shaking, his thumb stroked my palm, and his leg was rapidly bouncing up and down. This time however, our nerves were for an entirely different reason.

Chapter 11

June 27th, 2016
02.15am

The sound of Jack and Conor's voices woke me. I awoke
to find myself lying across a cold steel bench in the waiting room of the accident and emergency department of
St. James' hospital in town. Eager to hear if there was
any news on Ró's situation, I sat up and tuned in to the
conversation. Jack stood with his back to me, with an
empty paper coffee cup in his hand which he waved
from side to side as he relayed information to Conor,
who stood anxiously biting his thumb nail beside him.
"Thankfully I'm free now, just a minor concussion and a
few stitches on my lip, but I'm going to go back in to
him now. Honestly, you guys can go home, his parents
are going to bring him home when he's let out."
I watched Jack disappear through a set of bright white
double doors as Conor turned back around to me.
"Ah. You're awake." He sat down beside me, rested his
elbows on his knees and put his face in his hands. A long

yawn escaped his mouth. He turned to me and told me what he had just been told.

"Jack is fine. He's just here to stay with Ró."

I put my hand on his back and stroked him softly.

"And how is Ró doing?"

The brief pause before he continued was a sign it wasn't good news.

"He's out cold at the moment. He was awake for a while but he's drifting in and out of consciousness. The prick who attacked him managed to dislocate his shoulder. He landed badly on his back so he had to have a few stitches there."

I raised my hand to my mouth in shock. The thought of Ró lying passed out on his front in a hospital bed terrified me. He was my strong friend, I had rarely seen him vulnerable.

"Did they catch whoever did it, do you know?"

Conor let out a sarcastic laugh.

"Of course not. When the guards were called, the stupid little cowards ran."

I shook my head. The feeling of anger I had been burying began to resurface again.

"I'm really angry, Conor. There must be a way we can find them. Someone must have had a camera. There were loads at the party."

He stood up and slowly shook his head at me.

"Nah. These attacks happen every year around Pride. It's nothing new. The guards won't think twice about it."

His last sentence replayed in my head. *The guards won't think twice about it.*

I watched as Conor started pacing up and down the room and thought about what we should do. I thought back to how Ró behaved in a crisis. When I had been harassed, he was there for me. He listened and didn't judge, he even went and got some revenge on my bullies. True to his character, he had always gone above and beyond for me. I couldn't shake the feeling of helplessness as I thought about my best friend lying unconscious on that hospital bed, and that there was nothing I could do to help him.

"Do you want to stay?" Conor had stopped moving and was now turned to face me. I knew that he was tired, we had been there for a while.

"Yeah, I'll stay. You can go but I'll stay here. In case I'm needed for anything."

He sat back down on the bench beside me and put his arm around me, pulling me in to him.

"Don't be silly. I'll stay with you." I felt him kiss the side of my cheek. "I might need a little nap though."

I smiled. "Of course."

I let him rest his head on my lap and he spread his legs across the rest of the bench.

Hours passed as I sat there waiting to hear that Ró was safe to leave. I looked down and realised that my hands had were balled into two clenched fists. My anger was directed half at the gang that crashed a pride party to cause trouble, and half at the guards for failing to follow it up. I replayed the story over and over in my mind. I hated myself for my initial state of disbelief. How naïve I had been up until that point, to not realise that there was still homophobic hate crime happening around me. My sheltered little brain had assumed that once the law was passed to allow gay marriage, that it had solved everything and everyone was as welcoming and accepting as my little social circle. I was heartbroken to have had to learn the hard way of just how wrong I was.

June 27th, 2016
05.30am

After hours of staring through the small glass pane on the door, Ró finally emerged through the double doors with Jack by his side. His left arm was in a beige sling, securing his hand tightly to his opposite shoulder. His face still had the remnants of the face paint he had so carefully designed earlier. I had never seen him quite so expressionless. Jack cracked a half smile as they approached, Ró remained silent. He fell into my arms when they reached us and I silently held him for a long few moments. The sound of him sniffing on my shoulder revealed he was also in tears. Eventually, when we separated, I managed to find something to say.
"I am so sorry that I wasn't there. I was thinking about myself when I left early like that. I should have been there."

Ró smiled in acknowledgment, but didn't say anything. Conor chimed in to defend my point.

"Exactly. We should have stayed, I could have done something to stop them."

Ró laughed at that thought. I was glad he saw some humour in the situation. When he composed himself, his attitude changed and he eventually spoke.

"Ugh. I haven't had such a good sleep in years. And they even gave me meds so for the next week if anybody needs me, I'll be in a deep, deep slumber."

Our small circle shared a moment of half- hearted laughter at his comment. When the silence returned, I turned my attention over to Jack and Ró.

"How are you guys getting home? Are your parents coming?"

Jack nodded as they gestured towards the automatic doors that lead out to the carpark.

"My Mom is outside." Ró confirmed. "Thank you guys for staying, you really didn't have to."

I forced a half smile and nodded to him.

"I'll ring you tomorrow to check in."

With a sheepish wave with his good arm, they both

disappeared through the doors and into the thin summer rain.

"I think I'm all out of taxi money at this stage" Conor commented once we were alone again. "Do you fancy a walk back to mine?"

As I too was broke, we followed the map on my phone back to his house. As we were two overtired zombies, the conversation was minimal.

The rain didn't bother me, and I actually enjoyed walking through Dublin city while it was still asleep. No one but the odd cyclist was out, flocks of birds gathered in the middle of the roads, and the only sounds were the beeping traffic lights. We were walking along the canal, about five minutes away from his house when I started the conversation up again.

"Do you think the country will ever change?"

He seemed a little confused in his tired state.

"What do you mean?"

I went on to explain myself. "Well, just the fact that people are still thinking its ok to assault someone for being gay. And even more so that the guards weren't able to do anything about it."

He let out a deep sigh. "That's heavy." I looked at him so that he would continue and give his opinion on the subject. He went on "Well, to be honest, I think it is changing. Last year they couldn't even get married legally. It's hard to know when my country has never shown prejudice towards me. I'm sure it's the same for you."

My clouded brain and state of exhaustion probably caused my brutally honest answer that followed.

"Well, actually it has. For me, anyway."

He scoffed back at me. "Little Ellie from the south side of Dublin, coming from a private school? How has anyone ever shown you prejudice?"

It clicked with me then. The waitress from the café, the signs in the toilets of college, the protests, and whole the entire movement. I began to see where they were coming from.

"Remember I told you about my last sexual encounter?" His expression completely changed.

"You mean your rape ? I'd rather you not classify it as that."

"Yes, that." He nodded in agreement. " Well, I actually

fell pregnant as a result of that. There was nothing I could do, but travel to the UK to get out of the situation." He stopped walking and turned to me. "Are you serious?"

I shrugged.

"Yeah. Is that a problem?"

Five consecutive blinks stared back at me. "No. No, not at all. No. Just-" he trailed off. "did you ever consider having the baby?"

I started walking again. "Honestly, no. I wish that I did but I can't truthfully say I considered it properly. Maybe if it had been with someone else or as a result of something else then maybe, but, no. No, I knew deep down what I was going to do as soon as I found out."

He took my inside hand and held it tightly as we walked. "I'm so sorry Ellie. And travelling was really your only option? How did you even organise that by yourself?"

I blinked the tears away and shook my head.

"Ah. I just did. It was grand. I just think that it would have been an awful lot easier and made me feel a lot less like a criminal if I had the chance to do here. Or even if there had been some support or resources available."

He squeezed my hand again.

"I can't say I understand you, or can even begin to imagine what that was like, but I think you are incredible for going through that and coming out the other side ok." Breaking the gravity of the situation, his ginger cat walked up and greeted us as we approached his house. I was happy to stop to pick her up and bring her inside.

October 3rd, 2016

03.43pm

The sounds of frantic students tapping away at their laptop keyboards around me was extremely distracting. My empty white screen stared back at me as a reminder that I hadn't yet even begun my poetry assignment that was due the following week. Gradually, my fellow students had one by one closed down their laptops, and left, signalling their completion of the task.

I was good at the practical side of drama, I loved the exercises and workshops and playing different roles. Unfortunately for my grades, I was awful at the academic side of things. Our task was to write a poem that we would perform in front of the class as a monologue for grading as part of our credits for our 'academic writing' class. As I stared at my blank screen, a pang of regret hit me, for all of those classes I had ditched with Ró. Of course he pulled through and finished it hours ago, he always did. As usual, I was struggling. He had material to write about though. Since the attack a few months previous, he had been diving deep into his feelings and using this to draw inspiration and content for his classes. And as well he might.

I, on the other hand, had nothing to write about. The sound of another student leaving the library broke any focus I had and caused me to make the decision to take a break. I too closed my laptop, left it on my desk under the careful watch of the library security guard and went through the double doors.

Unfortunately, the sounds of roaring voices greeted me as I pushed open the thick brown door. A sea of faces and posters were pressed up against the gates, about twenty feet in front of me. As I pulled out my cigarette box, I walked slowly towards them. I had managed to avoid a repeal protest for a few months at that point, but I felt that this time, I would be less afraid of them. How wrong I was.

Images of severed bloody foetuses, and little babies' faces splattered with blood were being waved around by a crowd of middle aged men. As I drew closer, I saw a few women with "Love Both" posters. The two Os were looped together to create an 8, to signal their support for the eighth amendment. It was a clever logo.

After taking a deep breath, I lit my cigarette and pushed through the gates, with my head down and my lips pursed.

As I battled through the crowd, a leaflet was shoved into my face. The image of the foetus plastered across the front of it made my stomach turn.

"LOVE BOTH" was roared into my face by a young girl, about my age. Her wiry red hair framed her chubby freckled face badly.

"There are 200,000 abortions every year in the UK. Do you want to see 200,000 Irish babies murdered?"

I took the leaflet off her and scanned it. I wondered what

a questionable statistic had to do with her. I couldn't help but enquire.

"Aren't there, like 60 million people in the UK?" she stared blankly at me in response. I continued "And 5 million here?"

Her cheeks flushed pink as she crossed her arms.

"What's your point?"

"So surely there would be significantly less than 200,000 abortions per year in Ireland if this law were to be changed. I can't do the maths on the spot but that's roughly 20,000?"

She didn't acknowledge my point and hit me with another memorised statistic.

"Twelve Irish girls travel to the UK every day from Ireland to get an abortion. If it was to be brought in here, that would be twelve girls, multiplied by 365 days."

I handed her back her sheet.

"I think that only adds up to about four thousand. Your statistics are a little off."

I started to walk past the crowd and onto the road, but something made me turn back to her. I felt bad for killing her argument.

"Look, I haven't made my mind up about what I think about this whole thing. But don't you think that as you said, if its already happening already, it would be better to regulate it?"

She shook her head aggressively at me.

"There is no good reason to kill a child. Unborn or not. Not even in those extreme cases of rape that everyone likes to throw around. Like, it's not even that common."

In that moment, hearing another young woman around my age, dismiss my situation so carelessly and ignorantly, I made up my mind. I agreed with her in part. Yes, there was no good reason. Good reason. But there was a very bad and sinister reason. I had my own opinions about terminating pregnancy because someone wasn't careful enough. I had my own opinions about how developed a foetus should be. But those 'extreme rape cases' do happen. They were common. And that was a valid enough reason to do it. My eyes filled with tears as I forced a big smile at the protestor and calmly handed her back her flyer. Turning on my heels, I flicked my cigarette into the nearest gutter and crossed the street, going straight into the café opposite college.

As the little bell on the door rang to signal my entry, the waitress looked up at me and smiled.

"Table for one?" she approached me with her little note-pad.

I shook my head.

"I'll take that 'Repeal' badge now please."

October 10th, 2016
12.45pm.

My knees quivered with nerves, bouncing up and down as I sat outside the lecture theatre holding my poem. Ró was beside me, whispering his lines to himself.

The feelings are still raw,
Despite my healed jaw,
For the way that I am hasn't changed.

What good did it do
For your devilish crew,
To have my gay face rearranged?

He had read it to me a few nights previous, all twelve verses. Ró knew just how to captivate an audience, his stage presence was infectious. I was confident he would pass with a very high mark. My poem, I hadn't read to anyone. I was terrified of the reaction it would generate. After I bought my repeal hoodie in the café that day, I had gone straight back over to the library and written the poem in one sitting. Despite my best efforts during the week, I couldn't edit or tweak it. Nothing seemed to improve my writing.

"Do you want me to watch yours?"

Ró had folded away his poem and was finished psyching himself up for his performance. We had the option of staying for each other's performances or leaving.

"Sure, yeah. I don't think it'll make a difference really to be honest. It will probably suck either way." I had little faith in myself.

The lecturer opened the theatre door, and our small class of twenty filed one by one in to fill the tiered seats. As usual, we would be performing in alphabetical order, which put me first. My page shook as my trembling hands held it just in front of me. I walked down the steps and stood at the top of the class.

"In your own time." The lecturer prompted as I placed my sheet on the podium and tilted the microphone down towards my mouth. After the low murmur of the small crowd faded away, and each face turned to watch me, I cleared my throat, and began.

Chapter 12

January 25th, 2017
6.30pm.

The sky had starting to grow dark, and the rush hour traffic in Dublin city was at a complete stand still. Everywhere I looked, there were crowds of people in black jumpers lining the streets with banners and megaphones. The word REPEAL was printed across jumpers, banners, hats, badges and just about anything you could paint it on. Returning home from my first day back at college after Christmas, my journey had been seriously hindered as a result of the latest 'Repeal the Eighth' protest. Having had to already disembark from my bus and walk, I was not in the best of moods. The combination of the rain and the aggressive protest around me, made me quicken my pace. Living with these protests so frequently was an awkward position to be in; I agreed with them, I was on their side and if there was a vote I would vote yes. However, my primary focus at that time was graduating from my final year of college in the Summer.

Despite supporting it, the protest was a major inconvenience to my day. The bag on my back was heavy with books from the library and was also a contributing factor to my dour mood.

This was the fourth protest of the new year. They had become extremely frequent and disruptive and I was in two minds about it. Yes, it was important to gain attention and start conversations, but Dublin was beginning to feel like we were at war with each other, and each side was growing more and more aggressive with each demonstration. If it wasn't 'Repeal' protests, it was flyers and posters with slaughtered babies on them. I wanted the whole thing to be over.

I was at peace with overcoming my history with the subject, and had started to try putting it behind me and growing from it. However, it was extremely difficult to continue to do so with the constant reminders everywhere I turned. There was just something about the world around me debating a decision I had made that was causing me incredible anxiety and discomfort. I wondered how others in my situation felt.

As I walked through the rain, exhaling my cigarette into a thick cloud in front of me, familiar voices began to appear around me. Removing my headphones, I looked around to see if I could put a face to the familiar voices. My heart sank when I realised. My head whipped around to see Jessica and her boyfriend, with an army of friends, holding banners and chanting slogans along the crowd. I stopped and watched Jessica scream with the throng of protestors.

"Get your rosaries off my ovaries!"

Despite its clever rhyme, the slogan was clearly attempting to antagonise those that were opposed to repealing the eighth amendment. Most of them were strong supporters of the Catholic Church, hence the rosaries reference. The slogan was a bit of a low blow. It was the side of the movement I couldn't allow myself to get behind. A lot of protestors didn't realise that throwing digs at the opposition, instead of making clear arguments would lose our side respect and credibility and hinder the outcome.

There were so many things wrong with what I was witnessing Jessica doing. I found it hard to continue walking and ignore it, as the entire scene just didn't sit right with me. As the source of so much grief directed my way, I found it hard to believe Jessica was genuinely here protesting for the right reasons. It felt like she was joining a bandwagon, that anyone could jump on so they could be seen and heard. I figured this was more likely her reason to suddenly change her mind and get involved. Fuelled by anger, I took a deep breath and approached her.

"Jessica."

She stepped down off a large electricity box and stared at me. After a few awkward moments of examining my face, she realised who I was.

"Oh, Ellie! God, I didn't recognise you."

I was wearing a maroon woolly hat, with my short white hair barely peaking out from the bottom. Ró had cropped it right up to my ears this time. It was the only thing that had changed since we last met, so I figured there was no way she actually didn't recognise me. My expression was dead.

"Nice slogan." I suspected that she could sense the dry sarcasm in my voice. If she did, she ignored it.

"Yeah, we made posters. Do you want to-"

"It's funny how it didn't matter when they were my ovaries." I interrupted her before she could finish her sentence.

The discomfort in her fake smile was obvious as she nervously glanced around, hoping that no one could overhear the conversation.

"What are you talking about?"

I scanned her face. Her appearance hadn't changed at all. And evidently neither had her personality. I decided I wouldn't acknowledge the damage she caused to me or my car. The crowd of boys around her had each began to turn towards us to see the interaction. I recognised them from the video of them vandalising my car. Two of them were Ross's best friends. My tummy felt sick at the thought of him and I decided I wouldn't entertain them any longer. I responded to her ridiculous question.

"Nothing. You know just what I'm talking about, you're a big girl, you don't need me to tell you."

Her fake smile fell, and I saw her swallow. She knew exactly what I was referring to. Perhaps she was embarrassed of the way she behaved towards me in the past, or maybe she just didn't care about or realise the damage she caused. I wasn't going to give her the benefit of the doubt.

"We should go for a drink soon, catch up." I could see through her, I always could. It was clear to me that now that there was a whole movement starting surrounding something she poured so much hate into, she clearly wanted to back track and make amends. I had to conceal my inner smile as I remembered the expression that my Granny had for people like her;

She would run with the hare and hunt with the hounds.

I never truly understood it before, but now it finally clicked with me. She would do whatever she could to be seen to be on the side of whoever or whatever was popular. Three years ago, tormenting me was popular. Now, being on my side was. I didn't care for fickle friends, I had my own loyal ones.

"I'll pass. Enjoy the protest, Jessica."

Walking away before she could properly respond, I heard the group she had with her murmuring amongst themselves, no doubt about what I just said.

On my walk home, I analysed the interaction. Should I have appreciated her progress in her ways of thinking? Or held a grudge?

Regardless of their reasoning or intentions, I told myself that at least the money that they had each spent on their black Repeal sweatshirts was going to a good cause.

January 25th, 2017
7.05pm.

My key turned in the lock and I swung the front door open. Dumping my bag on the floor, I went straight to the kitchen to eat, I was starving.

"Ellie? Is that you?" I could hear my mother calling from the study. She emerged into the kitchen, only to grimace at my wet appearance.

"You did get stuck in a protest again? *Repeal*, really? Is there nothing else going on in the world?"

Ignoring her rhetorical question, I opened the fridge to inspect its contents, before closing it. I was disappointed. I could hear my mother try a different approach.

"How was college today? Did you get your work done?"
The work she was referring to was my thesis, and I had
been working away consistently at it for months, for
once I was on top of things.

"Yeah, I got some stuff done. I left a while ago though,
the protest on the way home kind of got in the way a
bit."

"A bit? They've been getting in the way of everything. It
seems every time I need to pop in to town for something,
the whole city is at a standstill because girls want to cut
their babies out."

I shot her a disapproving look.

"That's disgusting, Mom. Don't say that."

She rolled her eyes and continued. "That's what it is
though, when you think about it."

Our awkward shared silence hung in the air as she pottered around the kitchen beside me.

"Why are they saying it's their right? It's not my right.
Who thinks it's their right to do something like that? "
The microaggressions were becoming a semi regular
thing at this point. I had become used to giving her the
same answers on the subject over and over again. There

was a tension between us that surfaced whenever this subject was brought up. As it was all over the news, everyone was talking about it and there were frequent protests from both sides; it was unfortunately brought up in our house a lot.

"I think it's more to do with the fact that if someone is raped or if there are medical complications, then they should have the right to end the pregnancy. No one really wants to have an abortion, Mom. Why would anyone want to do that?"

Dismissing my explanation as usual, she muttered on about how it would become a form of contraception and how graphic and strange it was to have such a private issue all over the city. I agreed with her on that part, it was a very private issue, one that I didn't want to discuss with her or with anyone. We had been having the same conversation about it most days now, there wasn't really much else to talk about. When I realised she was still talking, I tuned back in to her ramblings.

"Anyway, it took us a decade to get divorce brought in. We may get used to it, they'll be screaming in the streets about abortions for years before there is anything done about it."

A male reporter's voice on the television interrupted our conversation when he mentioned the words "Repeal the Eighth campaign", which caught our attention. My mother stretched out her hand to turn the volume up on the remote.

"Here we go again now."

The face of Savita Halappanavar, an Indian woman living in Ireland who had died a few years previously from a 'medical misadventure' regarding her pregnancy, appeared on the screen. At that point, I wasn't aware of the full story.

" *A mural has been painted in South Dublin of Savita Halappanavar. Savita was an Indian woman who died in hospital here in Dublin, when an abortion was refused to her by medical staff…."*

My mother sat down on the arm of the couch in silence and hired the volume further.

".. Although she was just minutes away from a natural miscarriage, under the Irish law, they could not perform such a procedure as the foetal heartbeat was still present. On the 28th of October, 2012, Savita developed sepsis and later died. It is widely believed that if a procedure had been performed, this would have been avoided."

My mother's hand was now lifted to cover her mouth in shock, as she watched in disbelief at the Irish news.

"...Halappanavar entered the hospital that day expecting a miscarriage, but it was the miscarriage of justice in the Irish legal system, that ultimately caused her death. The people behind the Repeal the Eighth campaign are highlighting this situation as a reason to demand a change in our abortion laws."

The room fell silent as she switched off the television returned to her pottering around the kitchen.

"I remember that happening." She finally uttered, after a few minutes of silence. " I didn't realise the details, but I do remember it happening. It was awful."

I chewed on a piece of banana and stared at her, not wanting to engage in conversation.
"It's a little more complex an issue than people are giving it credit for. But what's to say we do end up getting a referendum and it will only specify that abortion should be allowed in these extreme cases?"
I swallowed my mouthful of banana.
"There's no saying that will happen, I guess. They're campaigning for a referendum and if it happens, it'll be up to the government to do what's best and remove the law, so that in these cases people don't die. "
She placed her hands on her hips and bit her lip, clearly thinking it through.
"But, do we really trust our government?"
I shook my head.
"It's not about trusting our government to make the right law. It's about getting them to remove a law that's

already in place. It's about giving women the right to then make the right choice for themselves."

She nodded slowly, blinking as she mulled it over to herself.

"So, it's not about trusting our government," she confirmed. "It's about trusting women."

June 14th, 2017

3pm

The heat was hot on our faces as we sat in Ró's front garden sipping warm cider. Having finished our last exam of college, we were engaging in a very tame celebrations, which involved Jack, Ró, Conor and I sunbathing in the rare sun. Jack returned from the kitchen with four ice pops, and we sat eating them peacefully. The radio played *Shape of You*.

I could feel Ró's stare.

"What?" I snapped at him, wondering what the fixation was.

"Your hair is getting a bit long again. It's almost at your shoulders at this point."

I rolled my eyes.

"Leave it alone. You are obsessed."

"What's the point in having a free hair stylist if you never let him at your head?" he hit back.

"I like it long." Conor pointed out. "I think you should leave it."

"Thank you *Conor*." Ró shrugged it off.

"Your loss."

Ed Sheeran faded out and the radio presenters voice started reading through the 3pm news. We listened as they revelled in shock at the unusually warm weather, before calling out the results of some sports match that no one in our little group was interested in.

"Change the station." I instructed Conor, who was sitting beside the speaker. He was about to do as he was told, when he stopped mid reach as the presenter mentioned the word 'referendum'.

The Taoiseach has announced that a referendum to see the eight amendment changed, will go ahead in Spring 2018.

All four of us froze like statues, I felt Ró and Conor staring at me, but I couldn't move. The radio presenter skipped past it and moved on to play another song, but I was still processing the news. A referendum was going to happen. This whole campaign had felt like my own personal nightmare being replayed in front of me over and over again, with just about everyone I knew chiming in their opinions. Now, there was an end date. Whether or not it would go through didn't matter to me at that moment, I was just comforted at the fact that it would all soon be over.

I snapped out of it and turned to the three faces looking over at me, unsure of my reaction. I didn't know what to say either.

"Fair play to the government on that one." Conor concluded when nobody else spoke. "I didn't know they had it in them." He raised his can of cheap cider and took a sip.

"Yeah." I cleared my throat. " Finally some real progress I guess."

August 25th, 2017
11.15am

"I just really think you should be involved, Elle. If it's something you believe in."
I hated when Ró was serious with me, mostly because he was usually right. This time, I wasn't so sure.
"But there's already a referendum. There's no need to keep campaigning."
I could see that he was getting frustrated with me, it was rare when we had a clash of opinion, but when we did one of us usually backed down. That morning, when I agreed to meet him and Jack for a coffee, I hadn't expected to be asked to go canvassing with them.
"That's ridiculous, it's not even close to being over. What if everyone votes no? We'll be right back where we started, and we'll have to go through it all again."
I didn't see the need to canvass. People had already made up their minds. There was still a large population

of Ireland who remained a part of the Catholic Church, and I didn't see them changing their opinions. He bundled the stacks of REPEAL leaflets into a tote bag, and handed one to Jack. They stood up from the table to leave, but before they did so, they turned to me.

"Are you 100% sure you don't want to come?"

He was almost pleading with me now, I didn't see how he could think it would be good for me to go. I sipped my coffee and nodded.

"I can't believe you of all people aren't taking this seriously, Elle. You can be a real pain in the ass sometimes."

He strutted out the door, leaving Jack still awkwardly standing at the table with me.

"He didn't mean that. He's just passionate about it because of what happened to you."

I shot him a half- hearted smile.

"I know. I just don't think I'm ready to debate my past with strangers going door to door just yet."

I could tell that he understood my point of view. I was wearing the my badge, that was my version of supporting the cause, and they both knew that deep down.

"I'll call you later?" he leaned down and kissed my cheek.

"Let me know how you guys get on." I called after him as he went to join an impatient Ró standing outside the café.

Chapter 13

November 18th, 2017
5pm

The speaker's words echoed through the white hall as I sat with Conor in silence, listening to her story. He could tell that the campaign war was taking its toll on me, and decided to take me to a peaceful gathering, where people spoke gently about their opinions. So far, a middle aged woman spoke about having her daughter at fifteen, and how her life had changed for the better since then, a man spoke about how his wife had to carry her baby who had passed away in the womb for weeks until it naturally expelled itself, and a young girl spoke about flying over to England after getting pregnant with her boyfriend.

Once they had each finished, everyone applauded and gathered at the back of the room for 'refreshments' and discussions. We decided to skip that part.

"Well." Conor prompted as we left the hall "What did you think?"

I could tell that this was his way of trying to help me, Ró

had been so involved in the 'Repeal' campaign that it was all he really talked about. It was interesting to hear the other side.

"Yeah, interesting. Felt so sorry for the guy whose wife had to carry her dead baby."

He shuddered.

"Yeah, that was awful. I couldn't even imagine what that was like for them both."

He held my hand as we walked towards the bus stop.

"Thanks for bringing me here tonight. I know it's not exactly how you'd normally spend your Saturday night."

He shrugged.

"I have no idea how to help you. I can't relate to your situation and I just want you to feel ok. I thought a calmer way of talking about things might help you process what's going on."

I smiled. "Thank you. I appreciate that."

He leaned in and kissed me as my bus approached.

"Do you want me to come and stay with you?"

I wasn't quite ready to let him go.

"Sure."

March 6th, 2018

5.45pm

"I think it would make a huge difference if you spoke. It's on International Women's Day."

Ró was on the other end of the phone, trying to convince me to speak at a rally. The referendum was two months later, and he had become heavily involved in the campaign.

"I don't know, does anyone really care about my story? I feel like I'd rather take a backseat to the whole thing. Whatever happens, happens."

"Oh come on Ellie, you know you don't truly believe that. It's in Dublin castle, there will be TV cameras there, it's being streamed on the internet and not to mention crowds of people. Think of all the people that could make their voting decision based off your story."

The thought of anyone I knew hearing me speak about body autonomy for women filled me with anxiety.

"I don't think so, imagine my parents saw. I don't want to sway anyone's decision with propaganda."

I could practically hear his eye roll on the other end of the phone.

"Are you serious? It's not propaganda. It's the truth. You don't even have to go into detail, you could just give your opinion. I'm tired of all these people standing up and talking about something they've never lived through. It's all so hypothetical. They need to hear from someone who has experienced it first-hand. Even if you don't want to tell them that."

His ramblings made sense. There was an awful lot of know-all campaigners who were speaking about something that for them was only ever hypothetical.

"Ok, look I'll think about it. Ok?"

March 8th, 2018- International Women's Day

6.30pm

I was trembling in the crowd. I couldn't make out if I knew anyone else here apart from Jack, Ró and Conor. Not letting go of his grip, I stood with Conor and breathed in deeply and purposefully. The nerves took over my body like I had never experienced before- I had never spoken in front of this many people before. I looked around- there must have been over a thousand here. My body had zoned out all the sounds around me. I couldn't make out what the speaker was saying, or what the crowd were shouting back. There were people in tears around me, most likely as a result of being moved by an emotional tragic story being told. Once I was up there, that was it. I could say that I did my part. People heard my story, probably the story of a lot of other girls who were too scared to tell it. I was scared too. Actually, I was terrified.

"You've got this." I heard Conor whisper in my ear as the crowd all politely clapped. Ró and Jack who were standing in front of me, turned around and smiled. Ró gave me a nod. I looked around, everyone was staring at me. It was my turn to speak.

Reluctantly letting go of Conor's hand, I walked up to the stage and slowly climbed up the steps. The crowd were still clapping. When I reached the podium, and took the microphone off the speaker, I looked out. I shouldn't have. Two large television cameras were no more than five feet away from me, pointing directly into my face. From up there, I had a view of the crowd. I could make out a few familiar faces. To the right, Jessica and her army of boys were all in uniformed Repeal jumpers. To my dismay, Ross was with them, also wearing the merchandise. Behind the camera men, I could see my college friends. To their left, my older brother stood between my parents. My eyes made their way full circle, to where I saw Jack and Conor standing smiling up at me. Ró met my gaze and cracked the biggest smile I had ever seen him sport. His hands were joined together over his mouth, as he nodded at me in support.

I spoke.

"Hi." The crowd murmured in response.

"Happy International Women's Day." I was interrupted by an applause. Once it died down, I continued.

"I recently graduation with a Drama degree, and one of my assignments during final year was to write and perform a poem." I paused. A few meek cheers from the back of the crowd filled the air.

"I got an A in the assignment, so I figured I would just read that instead of telling my story." Unfolding the piece of paper, I inhaled slowly, before reading my own words.

"From the moment I walked in and bought the test
I could tell it was bad news, I could feel it in my chest.
The father was sound and he promised he'd pay
This had to be a secret, he swore not to say.
Before I could even call my best friend,
It was all over Whatsapp, I had to contend
With people I didn't even know before
Saying I was a fake, I was a whore.

He turned on me then, following the rest
Saying I was a liar, an annoying pest.
Girls from school took his side, it was "fake" for "attention",
Saying ruining his life was my only intention.
We were never a couple, so that made me a slut
So HE was the victim , of the thing in MY gut.
"Did you not take your pill?" was their constant torment,
but I did take my pill- I was the 2 percent.

Then came the rumours, from the boarding school boys
Not realising how much of my soul they'd destroyed.
I had nothing left to fight for, not a clump or a cell
Half made up of me -half a boy from hell.

He made the decision with no hesitation
Then didn't even bother to show up at the station.
With 900 quid on a lend from my brother
I went up alone, didn't tell my mother.

It's painful and tiring and makes you feel sick-
Killing the innocent child of some prick
That wouldn't even look at me or say my name
That left me on my own and said I was to blame
He broke all his promises, he never paid
For his tiny and painful baby grenade.

But the pain of the procedure is not the worst part
Not the scars on my pride or the tears in my heart
But the failure of my country to give me the right
To stand up for myself, to not feel like a plight

To make a decision that's best for my health

Not hop on a train full of hate for myself

Not be a victim of stigma and hurt

Not a fugitive running or treated like dirt

But a girl who never even made a mistake

Who was a victim of rape and was forced to escape.

Eleven other girls did the same thing that day

Did they tell their moms? Did they run away?

Did they have someone with them? a lover? a friend?

A shoulder to cry on? or 900 to spend?

I made it back down on the last train that night

I missed my dinner, but they left on the light.

The very next morning I was up at nine

I hated myself , and I wanted to die

My Mom caught me crying, asked why would I bawl?

'It's my first day of college. Just nervous.

-That's All.' "

On 25 May 2018, the Irish people voted by 66.4% to 33.6% to repeal the Eighth Amendment.

Acknowledgments.

I would like to extend a huge thanks to my Mother, Susan, who read my first messy draft in one sitting, with much patience and little judgment. I'd also like to thank Max for constantly reminding me to write, Nick for helping me to brainstorm, and Sam for being a walking thesaurus.

Finally a big thank you to my Dad, Declan, for always supporting me and to Patrice for her motto;

"Never sell yourself short."

About the Author

Born in 1996, Sophie O'Neill grew up in South Dublin with her three brothers. Here she attended the Conservatory of Music and Drama, from where she graduated with a Musicology degree in 2018. Since then, she has been working as a music teacher full time in a private music school. This is her first novel.

Samaritans Ireland- <u>116 123</u>

Dublin Rape Crisis Centre- <u>1800 778 888</u>

Unplanned Pregnancy: HSE My Options- <u>1800 828 010</u>

Printed in Great Britain
by Amazon

49704571R00139